GRIZZLY MOON

GRIZZLY MOON

PATRICK DEAREN

FIVE STAR
A part of Gale, a Cengage Company

GALE
A Cengage Company

LIBRARY OF CONGRESS CATALOGING-IN-PUBLICATION DATA

Names: Dearen, Patrick, author.
Title: Grizzly moon / Patrick Dearen.
Description: First Edition. | Waterville, Maine : Five Star, a part of Gale, a Cengage Company, 2023. |
Identifiers: LCCN 2022026062 | ISBN 9798885781046 (hardcover)
Subjects: LCGFT: Novels.
Classification: LCC PS3554.E1752 G75 2023 | DDC 813/.54—dc23
LC record available at https://lccn.loc.gov/2022026062

First Edition. First Printing: February 2023
Find us on Facebook—https://www.facebook.com/FiveStarCengage
Visit our website—http://www.gale.cengage.com/fivestar
Contact Five Star Publishing at FiveStar@cengage.com

Printed in Mexico
Print Number: 1   Print Year: 2023

Dedicated to these masters of wilderness adventure:
Edgar Rice Burroughs
James Oliver Curwood
Jack London

CHAPTER ONE

"Who's there!"

Washington Baker raised his Colt Model 1878 shotgun against the ominous night as his challenge died in the growl of thunder. Thumbing back both hammers with a quick click-click, he seated the iron butt plate against his shoulder. He dug his index and middle fingers through the trigger guard and found the concave triggers ready to drive the hammers forward. In each side-by-side chamber waited a 12-gauge double-aught shell with nine .33-caliber pellets, a fearsome load sure to kill. He couldn't see the brass bead down the center rib of the 30-inch barrels, but he knew it was there, fixed against the shadowy form coming straight at him.

"Answer me!" he demanded. "Who's there!"

But the only reply was the rumble of thunder, and Wash squeezed both triggers in fear and panic.

Nineteen years had passed since that fateful night on the Middle Concho River in Texas in 1880, but in this hour in mid-November sixty-year-old Wash could still hear the 12-gauge's roar that had changed lives forever. He could still feel the recoil in his shoulder and taste the gun smoke hanging in the air. He could still feel the hot blood as he had swept his twelve-year-old son up in his arms, and in Wash's throat still hung the same desperate cry.

Who's there!

Wash had asked the question of the storm-wrenched darkness, and now he asked it of the midday clouds, showing through the overhead latticework of the sprawling brush arbor in the shadow of Sawtooth Mountain in the Davis range of Trans-Pecos Texas. On a weathered bench, he sat to the right of his wife, Emma, and their nineteen-year-old daughter, Grace, a family of three that should have been four, joining thirty other ranch families in the camp meeting's closing service at the Rockpile, a stand-alone heap of huge boulders in this high valley.

Answer me! Who's there!

His unvoiced cry to the sky seemed to roll through the bordering oaks and pinyon pines on the north and die in the tasajillo-dotted grassland beyond the boulders, while from the watching mountains on the eastern horizon came not even a mocking retort. Indeed, except for the rattle of the latticework in the wind, and the rustle of gray oak leaves through the arbor's open sides, the answer was the same as always since that tragic moment.

Silence.

But Emma still believed that someone looked down from on high, weaving events for His purposes, and as Wash lowered his gaze, he found Brother Isom Jones preaching on that very subject from an Arbuckle coffee crate at the front of the congregants.

" 'All things work together for good to them that love God,' " quoted Isom. The wind-tossed pages of an open Bible draped on either side of his supporting hand. He was a small, wiry man with a balding pate and a prematurely graying goatee, and the azure backdrop of the mountains accentuated the unhealthy pallor of his face.

"But if you don't love God enough to confess that heinous sin," Isom continued in his nasal whine, "He'll punish you in this world and burn you up in the next. You think you can run away from what you've done? It's like trying to escape your shadow. No matter which way you go, how fast you run, it still hangs on.

"That's sin, my friends. Confess it or you'll suffer."

Isom looked as if he knew what it was to suffer. He was only in his thirties, but behind steel-wire spectacles his dark eyes were as dead as those that stared back at Wash whenever he peered into a mirror. Wash, however, had the experience of two decades in coping with tragedy, while only eight months had passed for Isom.

Throughout the sermon, a gruff voice had punctuated important points with a loud "Amen!" Now, from two rows ahead of Wash, Ed Mulholland did so again. But what the hell did Mulholland know about suffering? The rancher sat between his wife and their thirty-year-old son, the latter a stark testament to the whims of cruel fate that had granted Mulholland an heir to carry on the family name while simultaneously denying Wash the same.

If the muzzle of Wash's shotgun had swung only inches to the side that stormy night, it would have been Wash sitting here with a son while Mulholland grieved a distant, lonely grave. Wash needed no other justification for now denying the existence of a caring God, although he always attended this weeklong meeting out of respect for Emma.

Well, for Emma and the annual hunt that concluded the get-together. Even now, his mind wandered past Isom to the farthest mountains and the knob of rock that crowned the highest peak at more than a mile and a half above sea level. Participants in the hunt usually bagged a few deer, and occasionally a black bear—the only species of bear ever found in the state, according to a recent report by a botanist.

But whether or not something deadlier had ever prowled the Texas night, fear could breed an outcome just as tragic.

Every so often during the service, Wash had seen the younger

Mulholland—Trey, he was called—steal a glance over his shoulder in Grace's direction. Only recently, Emma had reminded Wash that Grace was a woman now, in maturity if not in years, and that he should expect suitors to begin calling. Now, as Grace smiled back at Trey, Wash wondered if Emma knew something he didn't.

If Ed Mulholland's son had ideas about Grace, Wash would put a stop to it in a hurry. No Mulholland would ever touch *his* daughter.

Wash bowed his head for the closing prayer, but as Isom's pleas to the Almighty persisted, Wash checked again for flirting between Grace and Trey. On the other side of Emma's reverent profile, their daughter was in equally devout pose as her blonde hair fell across her cheek. But it was what Wash saw beyond Grace that seized his attention. Through the oak-and-pinyon grove, which extended to a ten-acre livestock trap at the grassland's edge, came a gangly figure that could only have been Tommy Blackburn.

The slow-witted man was forty now, and he seemed all arms and legs as he flailed wildly. Not since Tommy had rushed into camp on that long-ago trail drive had Wash seen him so panicked, and Isom cut short his prayer as Tommy neared with shouts of "Mr. Wash! Mr. Wash!"

Rising, Wash faced him over Emma and Grace as Tommy arrived breathless at the arbor.

"Mr. Wash! Mr. Wash!" Tommy repeated. His chest heaved as he bent over with hands on knees so that he was framed by two arbor posts. Tommy had lost his hat somewhere along the way, and his shock of red hair was as unkempt as a horse tail full of cockleburs.

"Mr. Wash! Mr. Wash!" Tommy's spittle peppered the dusty ground.

"I'm right here, Tommy. Look up at me and tell me what in

the Sam Hill's the matter."

Tommy complied, but his eyes were as wide as the circles with which he had helped trail-brand the combined herds of Wash, Mullholland, and Isom's father before they had pushed west for their respective new ranges in these mountains back in '80.

"I seen it. Just like that time where Kiowa Creek come in to the Concho, I seen it!"

Wash squeezed past Emma and Grace. "You's tremblin' all over, Tommy. Calm yourself down a little so you can talk."

Wash didn't know that Ed Mulholland had edged out on the same side until they bumped shoulders near a support post.

"Sure interrupted the prayin'," complained Mulholland, hoisting his belt so that his ample belly hung over it.

Dressed as slouchily as ever in a wrinkled woolen shirt with cigarette burns, the rancher looked older than his fifty-eight years, but Wash figured that was to be expected. After all, his nose, cheeks, and the V of the neck showed the red spider veins of a man who had emptied his share of bottles.

"Pretty disrespectful of your man, Baker," Mulholland told Wash.

Wash wondered which of the two was actually the disrespectful one. Mulholland was on the camp meeting board of trustees, and yet his eyes were inflamed and the rank odor of liquor hung over him.

"I suppose Tommy's got a right to his say," Wash said impatiently.

From behind came polite words. "Go ahead, Tommy."

Wash didn't look, but he recognized the soft voice as Trey's.

"Take your time," Trey added, "and tell Mr. Baker what it is."

Wash had never had any more use for Trey than for the elder Mulholland, not since that night on the trail, anyway. But Wash had to admit that Trey had always been understanding about Tommy's lot in life.

"You just got to see, Mr. Wash," managed Tommy. "You just got to see!"

"All right," said Wash, "but let's do it in a walk. I'm down in my knee with rheumatism."

Wash started after Tommy, only to find Ed Mulholland accompanying them uninvited. Glancing back at the crowd that stirred under the arbor, Wash saw Trey lingering—and Grace, with a smile on her face, approaching the young man in a way that said far too much to Wash's liking.

Wash relived the start of a nightmare that had never ended.

He was back at the Middle Concho-Kiowa confluence in 1880, and yet this was 1899. He was staring down at the partially devoured carcass of a speckled longhorn steer with a wide spread of mossy horns, and yet this was the remains of a short-horned milk Jersey he had trailed along at the length of a rope behind the wagon a week ago. He saw the long-ago steer's nose crushed on the side and its head twisted back at an impossible angle against its shoulder, and although the Jersey didn't have a longhorn's sinew, the milk cow's face had sustained similar damage and its neck was broken just as dramatically.

"I told you, Mr. Wash," Tommy said excitedly. "It was just like that mornin'. Look yonder where it come through the bobwire. Broke it all to pieces, sure done it."

They had pushed across open range nineteen years ago, but Wash saw what Tommy meant. A few yards to the left was a water hole, sparkling in the same sunlight that burnished the eighty-foot jumble of wagon-sized boulders immediately beyond. The rounded rocks were a natural barrier, and from it a fence extended into the grassland and formed the side of a trap that incorporated the pool and acres of grazing. Wash himself had helped stretch the four strands of barbed wire between stout, juniper posts thirty-three feet apart, and he had remarked at the time that worshippers would never have to worry about their cattle and horses breaking through.

And yet forty yards out from the boulders, the fence had been breached, the wire glinting in wicked coils beside a splintered post.

The ground about the carcass was disturbed, any clues impossible to read. But as Wash started for the breach, he picked up a trail and followed it to a point near the fence. As he knelt in inspection, he was back in the past again, tracing with a finger the outline of a track that now, as then, caused his jaw to drop.

"Ever' bit as big as the one on that cattle drive," Mulholland remarked from over Wash's shoulder.

The hind track resembled that of a man's bare foot, but it dwarfed even Wash's size eleven boot. Indeed, the imprint was more than a foot long from heel to claw marks. The pad, narrow and rounded at the heel, broadened to six inches near the five toes—a massive track that had flattened the soil underneath. The front track was smaller, perhaps seven inches long and five inches wide, but claw marks extended a full four inches from the toes.

Standing, Wash studied the span from hind track to hind track and determined a walking stride of five feet, twice that of a man. The gait, clearly of something four-footed, had peculiarities; a hind foot regularly overstepped the one in front, and as Wash traced the trail back toward the carcass, the stride lengthened, each track assuming a C shape in evident response to a lope.

"Look here."

Turning, Wash saw a kneeling Mulholland lay his open pocketknife across a track.

"See how square the front foot is?" Mullholland went on.

13

"Lay you a straight edge behind them toes and they's almost in a line. Ain't but one thing makes a track like that."

That's what Mulholland had told him back in '80. At the Concho-Kiowa confluence, with Tommy looking on just as he did now, Mulholland had told him that very thing. The rancher had laid his pocketknife across a track and filled Wash's mind with all sorts of notions, and in so doing he had set in motion all the events that had followed.

The bastard, it had been his fault! All of it, Mulholland's fault!

Returning with Tommy to the carcass, Wash stood considering the power that had crushed the nose and broken the neck.

"Slapped her left and right, quick as blazes." Mulholland was right behind Wash again. "That's how it kills, you know. Like sledgehammers, both sides."

Wash had heard it all before, all right. An eight-hundred-pound monster faster than a racehorse, more nimble than a tomcat, and stronger than a team of mules. *Better watch out come night*, Mulholland had warned. *Thing'll be on you before you know it. If you see somethin' comin' in the dark, shoot the damned thing or you's deader than hell.*

Death would have been better, thought Wash.

"Tracks goes from here plum' across trap, sure do," spoke up Tommy, pointing east. Seeded with green pinyons and junipers, the rolling valley unfurled for miles toward the range's loftiest section, prominent on the east horizon. "That's how come me to find ol' Jersey—I come to a broke place in the fence way yonder and followed ol' tracks back. I done good, Mr. Wash?"

"Awful good, Tommy," said Wash. He scanned the barbed coils beside the nearby breach. The wind had blown from the opposite direction during the night, and whatever had entered here must have lain in wait downwind while the Jersey had come in for water.

14

"Hants done this, Mr. Wash?" Tommy glanced about nervously. "They still be around?"

Ghosts, indeed. The ghosts of regret and loss that would haunt Wash the rest of his days.

"Got to track that thing down," said Mulholland. "Cattle killer, sure as hell, like what's up in Colorado. Same as I told you in eighty, Baker—a grizzly."

Yes, Mulholland had told him, and as Wash lifted his gaze to the trail that bore for the mountain heights, he recognized a chance to right that wrongful shot after all these years. It was a sudden obsession, but one no less powerful than an abrupt call to vengeance.

As his ears rang louder with that long-ago shotgun blast, Wash turned and glared at a father who still had a son.

CHAPTER TWO

The dark of the moon had made the long night all the more troubling, but Rosindo Mesa's cries at sunrise met with the same worrisome silence.

"Papá! Papá!"

From the cracked saddle of a roan horse, the eleven-year-old muchacho had called out in his native Spanish ever since riding away from their adobe home on the little stream hours before. Now that he neared his father's trapline in the wooded lower reach of the Fronterizas—an island range in northern Coahuila's Chihuahuan Desert—he shouted with an urgency that bordered on desperation.

"Papá! Where are you, Papá?"

Normally Rosindo would have gone with his father to collect the pelts, but nine-year-old Benita had taken ill and they had no mother to care for her. Their father should have been back by late morning, but as the early November sun of 1899 had crawled across the sky and sunk into the gleaming ripples upstream of their home, he had not returned. Whether with Rosindo or alone, he had never failed to ride in before dark, and as soon as Benita had improved in the night, Rosindo had set out west for the Fronterizas in search.

Now he brushed past the drooping greenery of a weeping juniper and faced a small clearing confined by pinyon pine and stunted gray oaks. A thick blend of milkweed, silk tassel, sage, and mahogany was like a wall under the surrounding limbs except in two places. Across and a little to the right, the trail threaded on, beaten by long weeks of horse travel in checking the traps. But the break on the left wasn't easily explained. The splintered limbs . . . the flattened stems of the shrubs . . . the disturbed ground that extended into the clearing. . . . It was as if something large and powerful had charged out of the vegetation.

Rosindo took his horse a few paces into the glade's subdued light and drew rein in sudden, paralyzing fear. Beyond the roan's ears, the turf was a battleground, the dirt and grass and rotting leaves churned and stained by something dark that could have been only one thing.

Papá! Papá!

Rosindo wanted to scream the words, but his voice no longer would work.

Shreds of white cotton clothing were everywhere, along with leather footwear and a sombrero. Across the clearing at eleven o'clock, a gnarly alligator juniper stood a few yards shy of the far vegetation, and a drag trail with the same reddish-brown discoloration extended past the tree's drip line.

Papá! Papá!

The morning wasn't cold, but never had Rosindo been so chilled as he dismounted. At his feet he found a Winchester Model 1890, a pump-action .22. He didn't want to recognize it, but as he took up the six-pound rifle, he remembered how his father had taught him to brace the walnut stock against his shoulder and take a bead down the 24-inch barrel. It had long been Rosindo's responsibility to shoot the live-trapped animals, and no matter what the consequences might have been, Rosindo wished he had been at his father's side this time as well.

He went on in a daze, leading the roan and avoiding the blood trail. When he reached the alligator juniper, he went lightheaded and clutched the scaly trunk for support. Just ahead was a mound of leaves and limbs that hid too much, and yet maybe not enough. An animal had cached something here, and as Rosindo shifted position to see through the branches, he pieced together enough of his dead father's features to throw himself back against the juniper and find his voice again—a wrenching cry that rose up from the wellsprings of the muchacho's heart.

He slid down the trunk, the rough bark scraping the hide from his spine. Yet he never flinched, not when he was so overcome by a different kind of pain, one greater than any he had ever known. In a world gone dark, he sat in stunned disbelief, a lost boy who didn't know where to turn. All he knew was that his *papá* was gone and would never come back.

Never!

Out of the depths of despair, he saw Benita alone at their adobe, and he found the strength and resolve to pull himself up and do what had to be done. Vigilant now with the Winchester, for her sake if not his own, he gathered heavy rocks and capped the cache so that it was secure from all but the largest animals. As he worked, he studied the scene and reconstructed the final moments of the father he had loved so much.

The day-old horse tracks, casually spaced, showed that his *papá* had entered the clearing unaware of danger. Several paces in, his pony had reared with him in startled reaction to something exploding from the brush. Before his father had been able to control the horse and flee, the predator had dragged him from the saddle. The sombrero and Winchester had gone flying, and as the pony had bolted down-trail without him, his father had been left to a terrible fate.

But it hadn't ended with his death. The predator had fed on the body and cached the remainder against the possibility of returning to feed again.

By size alone, the tracks were those of *el diablo*, a devil out of hell. Tipped by claw marks stretching several inches from the toes, the front prints were five inches wide and seven inches long, while the rear were much larger. His father had told Rosindo about finding such tracks once; *el oso plateado*, the silver bear, as he had called it, had passed through the Fronterizas in bearing north for the Rio Bravo del Norte, the Rio Grande. But that had been nineteen years ago, and never again had he seen evidence of *el oso plateado*.

Until it had been too late.

Rosindo secured his father's sombrero and trudged to his horse. Emotionally and physically drained, he barely had the strength to step up into the stirrup. Once he was seated, the animal spun with him and slung its head nervously, for the smell of the silver bear must have still been strong. With a forlorn sob and a look back through the alligator juniper at his father's grave, the muchacho turned the roan back up-trail and rode away through a heartless world.

He had to have help. He couldn't face the next moment, much less the rest of his life. His chin against his chest, he could only give the horse its head and rock with the animal's gait to the somber toll of the hoofbeats.

Rosindo never realized he had dozed off in the saddle until he awoke with a start. It had been a restless, troubling sleep, and darting images came with him out of his nightmares. The flashes were mainly of his father, dark apparitions bearing his unmistakable form even though shadows always veiled the face. His father seemed to beckon, urging Rosindo to return for some reason to the place of his death. But though the muchacho begged him to explain, the only response was an ominous silence.

For minutes or hours, Rosindo clung to the creaking saddle, a tortured boy drifting between sleep and wakefulness and unable to tell the difference. Eventually he became vaguely aware that his head nodded, but not until he heard chickens squawking did he grow alert.

Down past the roan's windswept mane, hens scattered from the hoofs as their red wattles shook against their throats. Looking up, Rosindo found himself on the outskirts of his small village, with the trickling stream on the right and a sagging adobe with cracked plaster on the left. This was the home of the *curandero*, the healer, and just past it Rosindo could see him stooped, tending his garden of herbs.

"Señor," appealed Rosindo as he approached. "I . . . I need help, señor."

Turning, the *curandero* straightened and squinted. He was the pueblo's oldest resident, a withered *viejo* with bent shoulders and a coppery face creased by the years. His long, white whiskers, as unkempt as his soiled cotton clothes, fluttered as he spoke.

"You do not look well, little one." There was concern in his quavering voice as he started for Rosindo. "Do I see *el susto* in your eyes?"

El susto. The fright. Indeed, *el susto* and more held Rosindo in its grip, so powerfully that it threatened to divide his spirit from his body.

The muchacho hunched over the saddle horn. "Help me," he whispered. "Por favor, please . . . help . . . me."

Rosindo began to slide down the horse's shoulder, and only the steadying hands of the *curandero* controlled his fall. Still, the ground surged up and the boy sprawled, the shifting hoofs in his face. Only through a haze did he grasp what came next: struggling to his feet to the tug of gnarled hands, his chin dropping, his leather huaraches shuffling beneath him as the bitter dust rose.

When awareness began to return, he was lying on an earthen floor in a shadowy room alive with the flicker of candles. He could smell resin burning in a nearby censer, and he winced as something that came from beyond his line of sight feathered across his face. He quickly realized that the old *curandero* brushed him head to toe with bunched stems.

"What are you doing, señor?" Rosindo asked.

"I must cleanse you with ocoxochitl and capsulin. Dried agave root too. Just rest, little one."

Rosindo tried to do so, but the *susto* was too great. Nevertheless, he remained on his back as the healer laid aside the stems and rubbed something white and oval down from the muchacho's hairline to his brow.

"Huevo?" Rosindo asked. "An egg?"

"From a setting hen."

The *curandero* must have just gathered it, for the egg was still hot as the skeletal fingers worked it on down under his chin. Rosindo could even feel the warmth as it contacted his white cotton shirt and passed on down his trousers to the bare skin between the leather straps of his huarache.

Twice more the *curandero* swept the egg the full length of Rosindo's body before drawing a transparent glass of water close. Curious, the muchacho watched the knotted fingers crack the egg and drop it inside. The yolk immediately sank to the bottom, where it stared out like a large yellow eyeball, strangely unsettling in its distortion.

With a candle, the *curandero* made a cross over the glass and invoked the names of Dios the Father, Jesucristo the Son, and Espiritu Santo, the Holy Spirit.

"Now we wait," said the healer, letting the glass rest on the floor.

Rosindo lay back, but he kept his face toward it. As the minutes passed, a change began to come over the egg's clear portion. It assumed the appearance of suspended white threads, like wispy clouds around a fiery sun. Then specks of blood developed, springing from the yolk until the muchacho could smell an unpleasant odor.

"*Madre de Dios!*" exclaimed the *curandero*.

Rosindo sat up quickly. "What is it, señor?"

"I read death." The old man turned, his eyes wide in the hollows under his brow. "You have seen death."

A sob hung in the boy's throat. "It's *mi papá. El oso plateado,* the great silver bear, killed him yesterday in the mountains. I've come back from burying him. All the way, I saw Papá, dressed in black. It was Papá, but his face was always in shadow. He was motioning back to the place he died, but he wouldn't tell me why. Help me, señor!"

The *curandero*'s features had gone ashen. "Your father—dead," he said in disbelief. "*Ay Dios,* now he is a *bulto!*"

"*Bulto?*" repeated Rosindo.

"A spirit not at rest, doomed to wander until a great wrong is made right so he might enter Heaven."

A shudder crawled down the muchacho's spine. "What great wrong could there be?"

The *curandero* lifted the glass so that Rosindo could see the yolk and ghostly strands of white backlighted by a candle across the room. For a full minute the *viejo* twisted the glass in examination, and then he looked again at Rosindo.

"*El oso plateado* fed on him in the dark of the moon, and the silver bear still stalks the nights."

"*Sí.* And the days."

"The bear has stolen away the part of him that gives the dead rest. Even now, *el oso plateado* grows stronger with it. By the next full moon, your *papá* will wander forever as a *bulto.*"

Rosindo dug his fingers into the *viejo*'s withered arm. "What can I do, *curandero?*"

"Your *papá* knows. That is why he beckons you back. No one else can help him."

"Por favor, tell me!"

Never had Rosindo felt such a piercing gaze.

"You must kill *el oso plateado*," said the *curandero*. "Before the next full moon rises an hour in the sky, kill the silver bear or it will be too late. No one else must do this—only you!"

Tiny Benita, riding double behind Rosindo, seemed to have no emotion yet unspent.

All through the night at their adobe, she had wailed her grief until the very walls had grieved with her. Their father had fashioned and laid every mud brick, and with their mother he had turned mud and straw into a home—a miracle possible only through love. *Sí*, Benita and Rosindo both had known their parents' love, or the pain would not have darkened even the sun as it rose swollen and fiery at their backs.

Rosindo faced it as he twisted in the saddle and checked his sister. Exhausted, she had finally lapsed into sleep, her head warm against his shoulder. There was something soothing about her arms clinging to him, for it reminded Rosindo of the great purpose that Jesucristo had set before him. Just as their father and mother had done for her, Rosindo would take care of Benita until Jesucristo gathered them all under his wings. In a place without tears, they would always be together—but only if Rosindo killed *el oso plateado* and freed his father's spirit to enter Heaven.

As it was now, every time Rosindo closed his eyes, he still saw the dark, faceless form that was their father's *bulto*, urging him on to the death place so the muchacho could track down and shoot the bear. To that end, back at the adobe, Rosindo had exchanged the .22 for his father's 1873 Winchester and a pouch of .44 cartridges. Tied to the saddle, the rusty carbine rode under his right leg, while elsewhere cotton sacks of supplies flopped with the horse's every pace. Lashed behind the cantle was woolen bedding, and already it must have provided insulation at Benita's back against the chill of the morning.

As Rosindo neared the clearing that had changed lives forever, he reached for the rifle. The silver bear had intended to return, or it would not have cached the body. Maybe if the saints smiled on Rosindo, he might ride upon *el oso plateado* and end things today. In revenge, perhaps he would skin the great bear with the knife at his hip and spread it over his father's grave.

With the rifle ready to shoulder, he broke upon the glade and found it empty. But there was something not right about the scene, and as the muchacho drew rein, he realized what it was. Past the limbs of the alligator juniper, the large rocks he had stacked on the grave had been disturbed.

Rosindo would have preferred that Benita stay asleep in case the remains had been exhumed. But when the two ceased to sway to the beat of the roan's hoofs, his sister lifted her head from his shoulder.

"Why are you stopping?" she asked. At his elbow appeared her small hand, pointing. "Is . . . Is that it, Rosindo? I want to give Papá what I brought him."

The muchacho scanned the surrounding brush, which looked no different than before. There was no indication that *el oso plateado* lay in wait, but their father probably had felt just as safe until the bear had charged. With Benita his responsibility, Rosindo would not let down his guard.

"Benita, there's something I must do first. But you have to cover your eyes with your hand."

"*Por qué?*"

"Promise me, my sister."

"But why?"

"Do it for Papá."

Once he confirmed that she had complied, he lifted his right leg over the pony's neck and dropped to the hoofs. Next, he helped the girl down and took her free hand.

"Remember your promise," Rosindo reminded her.

As he led her across the clearing, he kept his gaze down, for he was as loath to look on his father's lifeless eyes again as he was to allow his sister to see. But when the coarse trunk of the alligator juniper loomed at his knee, he steeled himself and raised his chin.

Rocks were scattered, shining in the sun, and something had been digging. The fresh tracks proved that it had been *el oso plateado,* but Rosindo's diligent work had evidently deterred even the great bear, for the grave hadn't been breached.

"It's all right, Benita. You can look, but stay with me and hold the rifle."

It wasn't easy, watching vigilantly for the bear while moving the heavy rocks back in place. Even worse, he saw everything with stinging eyes and heard Benita sobbing as she hung her head. Finally, however, a stony mound again protected their father's grave.

"Is it around your neck, Benita?" he asked.

She looked up. Benita was a pretty girl—as pretty as her mother, their *papá* had said—with long eyelashes and raven hair past her shoulders. Their mother had been one-quarter Indian, and Rosindo could see it in his sister's rounded face with high cheekbones and drooping nose.

The girl passed him the firearm, and upon reaching inside her white cotton blouse, she withdrew a small, silvery crucifix. As she slipped the chain over her head and extended it, Rosindo remembered their father presenting her the cross at her First Holy Communion.

"Where can Papá see it, Rosindo?" she asked. "When he looks down from Heaven with Mamá, where can he see it?"

Rosindo, too, would have been comforted by the thought of their father looking down at Jesucristo on the cross, but as the muchacho closed his eyes, the dark-shrouded form was there again, motioning him toward *el oso plateado*'s fresh trail. Benita seemed oblivious to the *bulto*, something for which Rosindo was thankful. He may have been only a youth himself, but he would shoulder the burden alone.

"Where, Rosindo?"

When Benita asked again, Rosindo glanced about. A limb of the alligator juniper extended to a point near the grave, and the muchacho went closer and reached up for it. Separating the hard, thin greenery, he worked the doubled chain over and passed the crucifix through the loop. Once tightened, the cross dangled free, the sunlight winking in its silver as it twisted in a gentle wind.

"He . . . He will like it there," said Benita, brushing her eyes. "Can we go home now?"

Rosindo wished they could. He wished they could return and find Papá waiting and realize this had all been a nightmare. But they couldn't.

He took the rifle from his sister. "Remember what I told you, Benita? What the *curandero* said about killing *el oso plateado* so Papá can rest? That's why we brought so much with us. We have to do it for Papá."

For a moment, she seemed to search for courage, and then her jaw grew firmer and she no longer sobbed. "*Sí*, I remember. For Papá."

They mounted up, and now it seemed to Rosindo that he no longer had to close his eyes to see his father's *bulto*. Assuredly, across the clearing the black figure, there and yet not there, ushered him toward the onward-threading horse trail—a trace profaned by the fresh tracks of a bear that must never see another full moon overhead.

CHAPTER THREE

Wash Baker couldn't look at the six dogs without thinking of his son.

On that drive back in '80, the big yellow mutt that Joe had raised from a pup had followed the chuck wagon all the way from Central Texas, and as soon as Wash had placed the last rock on his son's grave, the mongrel had lain beside it. The dog had rested its head between its paws and grieved the only way it had known how, and no amount of coaxing had made it rise. Finally Wash had ridden on with the herd, and even now he could almost hear the long, mournful howl that had gone with him.

In all these years, Wash had never been able to bear the presence of another dog. Yet now, from the general campground, approached Mulholland, leading a sorrel horse with four hounds roped to the stirrups. Trailing along behind the sorrel were two unsecured bull terriers, one brindle and the other white with black around the erect ears. The hounds had bayed incessantly every night of the meeting, and as Wash waited tired-eyed with his Appaloosa outside the repaired exit breach in the fence and dwelled on what lay ahead, he wished that they hadn't done so again in the predawn hours.

"Nobody be touchin' my dogs," said Mulholland. He must have just taken a nip, for the stale odor of liquor was stronger than before. "Tommy, I'm talkin' to you."

Wash glanced at Tommy, who stood holding a dapple gray

horse by the bridle, and his anger flared. He didn't know why Mulholland had singled out the slow-witted man.

"Tommy's nowhere near your dogs," Wash defended.

"Yeah, well, see to it your man keeps it that way. Traded a breeder in Tennessee four heifers for these bloodhounds. The bull terriers too. Been trainin' them just the way I want, so nobody be foolin' with them."

Wash didn't know who would care to have anything to do with something of Mulholland's. Certainly not Brother Isom, who was tightening the cinch of a bay horse just beyond the nose of Wash's Appaloosa. After one of the bloodhounds had chased a rabbit through the brush arbor one morning and disrupted Isom's preaching, the clergyman had issued strict instructions that all dogs be tied.

Of the four other individuals present—Wash, his daughter Grace, Tommy, and Mulholland's son—only Trey might have been disposed to take a role with the dogs. In fact, Wash could have wished it, considering how preoccupied Grace was with Trey. At her request, the sandy-haired man, lean in all the places that Mulholland wasn't, was busy adjusting her stirrups. Hell, Wash had rigged the roan for her himself.

"Can't wait around all day, way that sun's crossin' the sky," complained Mulholland, his words slurring a little. "Let's get on that bear's butt."

Sunset would come early, all right, but no one wished for extended daylight more than Wash, who had committed a great wrong that he needed to right, if only in small measure. He had been so eager to embark that he had regretted the long delay required to break camp so Emma and his roundup cook could start home with the other congregants who weren't participating in the hunt. Waiting around for Mulholland had added to his impatience, and he was about to make an intemperate remark when Trey looked up with raised eyebrows.

"Father, everyone gathered as planned forty minutes ago."

Considering who Trey's father was, Wash didn't know how the young man had learned such precise diction. From his schoolteacher mother, Wash supposed.

"Yeah, well, had to get them dogs fed," replied Mulholland.

Dismounting, he hitched the sorrel to a fence post and then set about releasing the bloodhounds. The nearest, weighing perhaps ninety pounds and standing thigh-high to Mulholland, was a tawny red with white on the chest and around the paws. The dark ears were floppy and long, hanging down past the droopy jowls. Most striking, the short-haired dog displayed the kind of wrinkles that would have made an old man seem young by comparison. Folds of skin hung loosely across the muscular frame and especially over the hazel eyes, giving the hound the appearance of being half asleep.

But the dog was very much awake, cringing at the approach of Mulholland's hand.

"Don't be pullin' away from me," Mulholland chastised. "Sleuth—what the hell kind of name is that for a dog? If I was drawin' up them registration papers, I'd've called you Clabberhead, the way you go off chasin' things."

As Mulholland freed the rope from the leather collar with brass buckle, Sleuth continued to cower and tremble—the sign of a dog repeatedly beaten, thought Wash. Already, he felt sorry for the animal.

The other hounds were no less fearful of Mulholland. Two were males with black and tan coats, one of them with a white-tipped tail, while the fourth dog was a reddish-brown female smaller than the rest. The female, Mulholland untied last, but he kept a firm grip on the collar and led her fifteen or twenty yards away from the fence where, Wash figured, the scents laid down by horses and people would only confuse.

"Let's see what kind of lead dog that old man traded me,"

Mulholland said as he released her. "Go on!"

At the command, the female placed her nose to the ground and started off on a zigzag course away from the barbed wire. Sleuth had picked up a scent trace of his own and was following it exuberantly north down the fence line, his hanging ears sweeping the ground on either side of his long muzzle. Wash couldn't help but wonder if he was trailing out the jackrabbit that the Appaloosa had scared up forty minutes ago. Sleuth must have been an old dog, for he favored a leg, but he was already a hundred yards away when the female bayed and took off at a full run with head up and curved tail high.

Sleuth responded, and considering the epithets Mulholland had hurled in the dog's direction, Wash knew that it was probably good that he did. Hobbled or not, the old hound quickly joined the other males in the chase, his cry more a croak than a bay. Meanwhile, the bull terriers, short-haired and two-thirds the size of the hounds, stayed with Mulholland as he mounted up. The terriers' massive jaws, thick necks, and deep-set eyes—small, triangular slits in oval heads—suggested a breed bred for fighting rather than tracking.

"Picked up ol' bear's trail, Mr. Wash!" Tommy said excitedly. "Runnin' off and leavin' us!"

"Expect we could hear them a good ways off, Tommy," said Wash.

But he was on a mission, and wincing to the rheumatism in his knee, he stepped up into the saddle and turned his horse after Mulholland, who, with the bull terriers, was already in pursuit of Sleuth and his swifter fellow hounds.

With his bedroll flopping behind the cantle of his saddle, Wash rode across undulating country spangled with juniper and pinyon. With every pace, he could feel the Colt Model 1878 shotgun in the slanting scabbard under his leg. It was the very Colt that he had wrongly discharged, its side-by-side chambers loaded with the same kind of double-aught buckshot that had plunged him into deepest hell with the twitch of his finger. If only he had tripped as he had scouted the stormy night . . . If only the ground had thrown the muzzles up under his chin . . . If only the roar in the dark had ended his own life and he had never faced Emma with news that no mother should hear . . .

Grace would have grown up without a father, all right, but at least she would have been spared a father so mired in regret that he had tried to mold her into the son he had killed. He had even taught her to ride astride in trousers rather than on a sidesaddle draped with her skirt. She deserved better, much better. But as he glanced back past Tommy to find her on drag at Trey's side, as if completely absorbed with him, Wash knew that it damned sure wasn't Mulholland's son that she deserved.

That night in '80 just wouldn't go away, but maybe Wash could at least deaden the pain the next time he braced the butt of his shotgun against his shoulder. Strangely, the image that he could see in his mind down the sights was not one image but two—a bear and a man, so closely entwined that he couldn't tell them apart.

He gigged his horse up alongside Isom to gain an unobstructed view of Mulholland, moments before the bastard's sorrel carried him out of sight behind the greenery.

Isom, on Wash's right, was muttering to himself and drew Wash's attention. The words were indistinguishable, but Wash read the trembling lips well enough to make out the name of the clergyman's late wife. Indeed, Isom whispered it again and again.

Wash was glad for something to distract his own troubled thoughts. "Been what—seven or eight months now?"

Isom looked at him with those lifeless eyes. Now Wash wished he hadn't broached the subject; he supposed both of them could see again the poor woman's body laid out on the eating table in preparation for burial while the newborn wailed in the night.

When Isom's stare lingered, Wash groped for something to say.

"Enjoyed your preachin' this week," he managed. In fact, the reverend wore the same black cutaway coat in which he had preached every day.

Still, Isom only looked at him.

"You never come huntin' with us before," Wash added. "Expect we might see some wild country."

The oval lenses of Isom's steel-wire spectacles, catching the sun's glare, stayed fixed on Wash.

"Listen to those dogs take on," said Wash, checking the way ahead over his Appaloosa's ears. Indeed, with four hounds on the chase, the baying was almost constant. "You know, I—"

"I can still hear the child crying, Brother Baker."

Wash faced him.

"He was crying," Isom went on, "and then he wasn't crying ever again."

Wash winced at an abrupt sensation of his fingers squeezing the double-barrel's triggers. "Least, your son died natural."

The moment he said it, Wash wished that he hadn't. Damn, he hadn't intended to make this about himself.

"I . . . I'm glad we give the poor little thing a good buryin'," Wash quickly added. "There beside his ma."

Behind the spectacles, Isom's eyes had begun to well. "The dirt was still fresh on my Lela's grave."

"I imagine the two of them will rest better side by side, seein' as how she never got to hold him."

Isom turned away and his nasal voice began to crack. "Two weeks. That . . . That's all he lived. Two . . ."

The frail clergyman's emotion kindled anew all of Wash's unsettled issues.

"I failed them," said Isom. "I failed them both."

For a moment, Wash's own voice wouldn't work. "I know it's been hard on you. I just know it has. But there wasn't a thing anybody could've did for either one of them."

When Isom turned again, his features were even more ashen than before. It was the kind of pallor that Wash had seen in the face of the innocent baby who had been denied a life everyone deserved.

"I . . . I never sleep anymore, Brother Baker. I close my eyes and all I can see is my Lela. All I hear is the child crying, and then not crying anymore."

Twice, Wash tried to speak before he succeeded. "I'm not anybody to be givin' advice to a preacher," he said quietly. "But from a old man to a young one, all we can do is go on and do the best we can. If we don't, we just sink deeper and deeper."

Which was what Wash had been doing all these years.

"Mr. Wash! Mr. Wash!"

Tommy was riding up on Wash's left.

"Ain't this somethin', Mr. Wash? Just like where Kiowa come into the Concho. We's all here—Mr. Grizzly and me and you, and Mr. Mulholland and little Trey all growed up. Course, Mr. Isom's done dead, but Brother Isom's took his pappy's place. It's like we's back there all over again!"

Tommy's hat was askew and his tangled red hair fell across his freckled forehead. In his excitement, his eyes seemed more crossed than ever, and as the words spat from his perpetually twisted mouth, Wash leaned back to avoid the shower of saliva.

"Ain't this somethin'!" Tommy repeated.

Wash would never have upbraided Tommy, who, he supposed, was reacting the only way he knew how. Indeed, all the significant parties from that trail drive were together again, except for Wash's son and Isom's father, who had died long after establishing a ranch near Fort Davis with his part of the herd. But Wash wished that this child in a man's body wasn't so oblivious to the dynamics at play.

Surprisingly, Isom didn't show restraint either.

"You needn't act so gleeful," he said.

When Wash looked at Isom, the clergyman's eyebrows were knotted.

"Tommy don't mean nothin' by it, Brother Isom," said Wash. "It's just his way."

Isom's jaw tightened. " 'There is a way which seemeth right unto a man,' " he quoted, " 'but the end thereof are the ways of death.' "

When Wash checked Tommy, blazed against a passing alligator juniper, he found the cockeyed orbs wide and the jaw slack.

"He sayin' I'm a-fixin' to die, Mr. Wash?" Tommy asked.

"No, course not. That's not what it means at all."

Tommy's features relaxed. "What *does* it mean, Brother Isom?"

Wash was afraid how Isom might respond, so he spoke up. "Ever hear anything like those dogs, Tommy? Used to take that yellow hound coon huntin' with Joe, and that ol' dog would . . ."

Joe.

Wash would rather Isom chastise Tommy than hear himself dredge up a story about his son.

"Preacher Isom," Tommy persisted, "what *does* it mean, what you said?"

Again, Wash broke in. "He's hurtin' right now. Let's leave him alone for a little bit."

Tommy cocked his head. "You got you a pain?" he asked Isom. "Ol' mule kicked me in the leg one time and I put axle grease on it. Sure done some good. We get back, you might try—"

"Maybe he can do that, Tommy," interrupted Wash. "How's that dapple gray of yours this mornin'? As spirited as ever?"

Tommy patted the animal's neck proudly. He may not have

34

had much in the way of smarts and would never be a top hand, but he was good with horses.

"Get along good, me and ol' dapple gray do. We's like two peas in a pod, couple of dogies our mamas didn't want no part of."

Wash knew all about it. One had been a foal rejected by a mare, and the other a doorstep baby shuffled from family to family until Wash had taken pity and hired him as a fourteen-year-old on the original ranch in Central Texas. Tommy, in fact, had been a godsend, for Emma had assuaged her grief by focusing on this kind soul who would never grow out of the boyhood in which Joe would always be frozen in memory.

If only Tommy knew the right thing to say and when to say nothing at all.

"Yes, sir, Mr. Wash, we's all together again."

Tommy just wouldn't let it go.

"Course, Little Miss wasn't borned then," Tommy continued. As if reminded, he glanced over his shoulder. "Say, ain't she takin' on over Little Trey."

Wash looked back at Grace for himself. If even Tommy had noticed, then "Little Trey"—as Tommy had called him since the cattle drive—damned sure needed reining in.

Grace wished that Trey wasn't Ed Mulholland's son.

Until recently, Trey had always been a distant figure, a grown man as far back as she could remember. Not only that, she had always heard her father speak of the Mullhollands in the most disrespectful terms. Indeed, he had used profanity in her presence just twice, and both times had been in reference to the Mulhollands. On the second instance, Grace's mother had berated him so strongly that he had never done so again.

Still, her mother's admonition hadn't erased hazy recollections out of Grace's earliest memories. Maybe they had been only dreams, these flashing images of a too-heavy revolver in her small hands as her father knelt beside her with instructions laced with something more troubling than a swear word. After so many years, Grace couldn't put all the fleeting sensations together, although she had experienced new details with increasing frequency ever since she and Trey had discreetly begun courting. That was what worried her, for right before the six-shooter of her dream-memory roared, she seemed to hear with the ears of a small child her own voice repeat what her father had whispered in rage.

Ed Mulholland!

Whether the recollections were real or imagined, there was no denying her father's dislike of the family.

Grace had gleaned enough clues over the years to suspect that it had something to do with the loss of Joe, although neither of her parents would speak of the night he had died. All she knew was that it had happened on the drive west with the pooled herds of the two families and Brother Isom's father. Whatever the Mulhollands' role in the tragedy, the attention Trey had paid Grace in recent weeks placed her in a position in which she didn't know how to respond.

She wanted to like him. She *did* like him. He was soft-spoken and polite, respectful and engaging, and he treated Tommy Blackburn the way the less fortunate deserved.

Trey was everything his father was not.

In her limited time around the elder Mulholland, she had found him loud, obnoxious, and overbearing, and it was little wonder that her father held him in disdain, even apart from whatever had happened on that drive. But Mrs. Mulholland, her onetime teacher, was unquestionably nice, and Trey fortunately had taken after her.

Nevertheless, that didn't ease Grace's guilt for enjoying the interest that Trey showed her. Strangely, though, ever since she had led her roan to the gathering point outside the trap, he had seemed reserved, even sullen, and now, abreast on her right, he rocked in the saddle with chin down and shoulders sagging.

"What's the matter this afternoon?" she asked. "You seem so far away."

He looked at her, the brim of his Stetson shading furrows that no brow of one so young should have. "Do I?"

"You wasn't this way at preaching."

"Well, I guess . . . Some things on my mind."

"What kind of things?"

Already, she felt she knew him well enough to press. After all, he had kissed her the evening before at the Rockpile boulder bearing the inscription *Kit Carson.*

"Long time ago," he said, shaking his head. "The more years I get under my belt, the more I think on it. With what's going on, being with you makes it worse."

Grace had never known that mere words could hurt so much, and she pulled the roan out of its jog-trot.

"You don't have to ride with me on my account," she said.

Trey slowed his own horse so that they stayed shoulder to shoulder. "I didn't mean it that way. I want to ride with you."

"You don't sound like it." Her temper had gotten the best of her, and she urged the roan back into its previous gait and wouldn't look over as he came up alongside and spoke.

"If you knew what I was dealing with, you'd understand."

"I heard plain enough. Just let me ride by myself."

For a while, he did, dropping back until his dun's hoofbeats were almost lost in those of her roan. But as the minutes wore on and the trail veered for Sawtooth Mountain, she didn't feel any better. On the contrary, she was in misery. Trey was her first real suitor, and this quickly she had gotten hurt.

Maybe Papa's right. Maybe Trey's just as no account as his—

"Miss Grace."

Abruptly the young man was at her side once more, drawing her focus. This time, he had removed his sweat-stained hat, and now he held it respectfully against the buttons of his linsey-woolsey shirt.

"I'm sorry, ma'am. I'm just . . . sorry."

When she didn't respond, he fell off the pace again, leaving her to ponder all that he had said.

But the dogs wouldn't let her reflect for long. Caught up in her exchange with Trey, she hadn't noticed that they seemed to bay less than before, as if three hounds were on the trail and not four. Then came a yelp, and she broke upon a stretch of wavy grama grass to see her father, Isom, and Tommy pulling rein before Ed Mulholland and the hound named Sleuth, who had clearly given up the chase. Mulholland was down off his horse, and he held Sleuth by the collar and lashed the cowering dog with a quirt. Meanwhile, the bull terriers, maybe all too familiar with the whip, had withdrawn a safe distance to the far side of the sorrel.

"Come back on me, will you?" said Mulholland, striking Sleuth again. "I'll teach you!"

"Mulholland!" The voice of Grace's father was rife with controlled anger. "Dog probably never picked up a scent like this before."

"Man said them hounds hunted bear all over Kentucky."

"You said this was a grizzly. The smell's got him scared."

Mullholland glanced back with a scowl. "*My* dogs. I'll train 'em like I see fit."

Across the stirrup-high grama fell one last shadow track—that of a crooked arm drawing back and snapping forward, whipping the rawhide braids of a bone-handled quirt across the cringing hound's baggy hide. Then Mulholland dragged the whimpering dog erect and pointed down-trail.

"Now go on!"

When Sleuth hesitated at the command, Mulholland kicked him in the hip and the hound slunk away, his tail tucked as he trembled and looked back furtively.

Mulholland brandished the quirt. "You want some more of this? Go on!"

Sleuth must have feared Mulholland more than whatever had laid down the powerful scent. With head up and tail arched high, he resumed the chase, hobbling more than ever through the tall grama.

"Old dog like that's probably got more aches that I do," said Grace's father. It seemed to be a measured way of asking Mulholland to spare the quirt next time.

"Even a old bloodhound can run twenty or thirty mile 'fore wearin' down." Mulholland lifted his gaze to the southwest, apparently checking above the bordering pinyons. "Looks of things, dogs'll have that bear tracked down *muchas* quick. Take a gander at where they's leadin' us. Them grizzlies like craggy mountaintops."

Through the windswept limbs of a pinyon, Grace looked for herself. If any peak around fit that description, it was Sawtooth, which rose almost two thousand feet from the valley. From the upper reaches of a demanding slope green with timber, compacted towers of rock sprang up several hundred vertical feet to a half-mile hogback, dramatically serrated and marked by slide corridors. To all appearances, the mountain was indeed a gap-toothed saw, blazed in the blue of the sky.

Mulholland mounted up and, with the bull terriers running alongside, loped his sorrel away through the pinyons and junipers beyond the clearing. Wash, Isom, and Tommy followed, and even from Grace's position a few horse lengths behind them, she could tell by the wild way Tommy sat his saddle and flailed his arms that he was upset.

"Ain't right, it ain't, it ain't," he railed. "Mr. Wash, he

whipped that dog somethin' terrible."

"I know he did, Tommy."

"Ain't right, just ain't right."

Grace had never heard Tommy so distressed, and he had been a presence all her life.

"Try not to think about it," her father told him.

"Ain't right, ain't right. Poor thing was cryin' like I done, Mr. Wash. They took a quirt to me same way 'fore you give me my job."

Witnessing Tommy's reaction was heartbreaking, but from over her shoulder, Grace heard something just as concerning.

"Know how he feels."

Trey said it so quietly that he may not have realized that he spoke aloud, and when she twisted around, his parted lips and flushed face confirmed it. Immediately he averted his eyes—pained eyes, she thought, accentuated by drooping eyebrows—and she straightened in the saddle and rode on, allowing him the privacy he clearly wanted.

Grace grappled with what to say, or whether to say anything at all. She hadn't made up her mind when Tommy dropped back alongside on her left.

"You seen what he done to that old dog?" he asked. "He sure a mean man."

He seemed oblivious to the fact that Mulholland's son rode only two horse lengths behind, but maybe Tommy's assessment wasn't anything that Trey didn't already know.

Grace did her best to be diplomatic. "We all have different ways of doing things, Tommy."

"He my dog, I never would beat poor thing." He patted the dapple gray's neck. "My horse neither. Your papa say, 'Show me somebody good to horses, and I show you a good man.' He sure right, Little Miss."

Tommy looked back with a squeak of saddle leather. Too

quickly for Grace to intercede, he asked Trey the very question against which prudence warned.

"Your daddy mean like that to you, Little Trey?"

All Grace could do was speak up. "Tommy, there's some things you shouldn't ever ask a person."

But Tommy couldn't be deterred.

"He take a quirt to your hide?" he pressed. "I yelp like that poor ol' dog ever' time they whipped me. You go to cryin' too, Little Trey?"

Grace couldn't imagine how Trey would respond. With dead silence? Or if he did address Tommy, would it be with gentle correction, or an angry outburst?

When Trey did reply, he spoke slowly, hoarsely, as if trying to maintain his composure. "Try not to let things upset you so much, Tommy."

But as soon as he said it, Trey bent his head and slumped in the saddle, as if struck by the realization that he couldn't heed his own advice with respect to whatever troubled him.

CHAPTER FOUR

The baying of the hounds echoed from the looming mountain heights.

Riding a little behind Mulholland and the bull terriers, but ahead of Isom and the others, Wash neared the limit to which his Appaloosa could carry him up through the big pinyons. The hoofs already were slipping in the rubble, and soon the horse would be able to advance only in lunges through the slapping limbs. Ahead, Wash could see the crowns of lofty ponderosa pines in the lower reaches of a brutally steep canyon, but they were dwarfed left and right by the enormous columns of rock that defined the middle gunsight in the summit ridge.

It all reminded Wash of how trifling he was. His efforts and aspirations, his accomplishments and failures, even his crippling guilt and regret. . . . Did any of it matter in the face of forces that had forged this mountain? He was just a pitiful little figure, lurching through life and unwilling to accept that nothing would bring back his son.

Nothing!

So why push his horse farther up this slope? Why go through another day, another moment, with one foot already in hell? Was there really a reason, other than Emma and Grace?

Through the strafing limbs of an alligator juniper, he glimpsed Mulholland dismounting at a hewn boulder taller than his sorrel, and Wash had his answer. Fueled by the track of a grizzly spanning the years, hate and vengeance could carry a man a long way.

Within a couple of minutes, Wash too had gained the boulder and was swinging off his horse just to the left of it. Tying the reins to the same scrub gray oak to which Mulholland's sorrel was hitched, he slid his Colt Model 1878 shotgun out of its saddle boot and studied it for what must have been several minutes, reliving everything in the curve of the hammers and delicate triggers. What would Joe have done with the life that Wash had denied him? Would he be a father himself now, hoisting his young son into the saddle in front of him? What dreams and hopes and grandchildren had died with him that night?

With a half sob, Wash planted a hand against the ochre-stained boulder and boosted himself up the slope through a stiff wind that tugged at his hat. He had a lot of questions for which he had no answers, and now he added one more—whether each step farther would carry him closer to some kind of resolution, or mire him deeper in perdition.

"Brother Baker."

Wash didn't want company at a time like this, but at Isom's hail from behind, he dug the edge of his boot into the unstable rubble and looked back. Down and away, between the two hitched horses, the clergyman and his white-lathered bay had almost reached the boulder.

"I can hear the child crying, Brother Baker."

Soughing from the high crags, the wind did have a mournful wail to it, enough for a troubled man to hear all sorts of things.

"Just the wind, Brother Isom. That's all—just the wind."

"I hear him like it was that day again. He killed my Lela and he just kept crying. He *killed* her, Brother Baker. My Lela, he . . ."

Wash stared at him. *What an odd thing for a man to say, even if it's true.*

"You can't let yourself go to thinkin' like that," said Wash. "You lose somebody, your insides can get all twisted up to where you can't think straight."

"But he *did* kill her, just being born. And there I was, just me to look after him, hearing him day in and day out. I can still hear him crying and crying and . . ."

Wash may have had unresolved matters, but Isom clearly had a bushel basketful of his own, enough for Wash to feel a twinge of guilt for being self-absorbed.

"I'm not anybody to be talkin', but you just got to snap out of it," Wash told him. "There's nothin' but the wind moanin' and the dogs takin' on. Way they seem to be bayin' nearly in one place, they might be close to corralin' that bear. Not a minute too soon, neither—the day's gettin' away from us. Hitch your horse there beside mine and grab your gun."

"I've never loaded it."

"You haven't?" Wash glanced at the gun stock showing alongside the fender of Isom's saddle. "Not much set on huntin'?"

"The thing I hunt for can't be found at the muzzle of a gun, Brother Baker."

Wash understood, or at least he figured he did. "Guess ever' man's got his own way of tryin' to find a little peace."

But maybe that's not what Isom had meant at all, considering what the clergyman said after drawing rein alongside the other horses and staring down at his saddle horn.

"They mocked Elisha." Isom's lips trembled with every word. " 'Go up, thou bald head, go up!' "

Wash had heard Isom preach on the subject at the meeting's opening service. Elijah had been whisked up into the clouds—or so the story went—and children taunted sparsely haired Elisha to do the same.

"He cursed them in the name of Almighty Jehovah," continued Isom, "and two she bears came out of the woods and mauled forty and two of them."

The remark was enough for Wash to give a cautious glance over his shoulder. "Hearin' you tell it, second time now, sets a pretty awful picture in your mind."

Isom looked up, the sunlight catching a glistening trickle from beneath the steel-wire frame of his spectacles. "Judgment. That was Jehovah's purpose for a bear—an agent of judgment."

For a moment, all Wash could do was study Isom's wan features. Wash's concern lingered as the clergyman removed the wire hooks of his spectacles from his ears and drew a knuckle across the hollow of first one moist eye, and then the other.

"I . . ." Wash didn't even know what he was about to say to Isom, for from above came the vicious barking of the bull terriers—as though Mulholland had set them on the chase.

Wash spun to the cliffs beyond the tops of the ponderosas. "They's about got somethin'. Or somethin's about to get *them*. If you's comin' with me, stay a safe distance back, case somethin' goes wrong."

Or maybe that was just the thing for which Isom hunted.

Through lengthening shadows, Wash climbed onward, his boots slipping and the thin air taxing his lungs. The rheumatism in his knee dealt him misery, but the building ache throughout his legs was even worse as he worked his way up through knurly pinyons. At another big boulder, he bent over with a hand on his thigh, every fiber of his being screaming *No more! No more!* before he could push on. And so the ascent went: climb a few brutal steps, pause, and climb again once his chest stopped heaving and the pain in his leg muscles relented.

Isom, somewhere behind, was forgotten in Wash's single-minded focus, for now he was driven not merely by hate and vengeance, but by pride. If Mulholland—fleshy and only a couple of years younger—could make this climb, then Wash

45

damned sure could as well.

Navigating a narrow gap between more great boulders, he broke onto an even steeper stretch up through scattered ponderosas that rose tall and straight against the cliffs' dark backdrop. Rock fragments rendered footing even more treacherous, forcing Wash to proceed with a hand on the talus. Gaining the first big ponderosa, he held to it and perched in exhaustion, tasting the pine's fresh scent and feeling its sap sticky against his fingers. Startled by the drum of nearby hoofs, he turned to find only empty slope and realized that he heard the hammer of his own heart.

Pride or not, he didn't think he could go another step, but as he scanned the way ahead, he glimpsed movement at the base of the second ponderosa above him. It was an arm, weakly rising from the ground in evident summons.

"Mulholland?" called Wash.

The arm dropped limply, and spent or not, Wash stumbled higher, responding to a man in need even as sinister thoughts rose up from a dark corner of his mind. The last few yards he accomplished only by extreme effort and then he was there, sinking to his knees in a mat of pine needles. Mulholland was supine, his flushed face beaded with sweat and his breathing rapid and shallow.

"I'm dyin', Baker." Mulholland's gasping words were all but lost in the cry of the dogs and the murmur of wind in the overhead limbs. "I . . . I mean it. Dyin'."

Nevertheless, there didn't seem anything wrong with Mulholland that rest couldn't cure. Wash's diagnosis was confirmed a few minutes later after a dog whined from the mountainside above and the two of them turned to find Sleuth approaching in a submissive creep with saliva dripping from his mouth.

"That good-for-nothin' hound!" Now Mulholland had energy enough to add a choice epithet. "Come back again, did you?" A dead pine branch lay between him and the dog, and he extended his arm but couldn't reach it. "Baker, grab that stick and beat the hell out of him for me."

"Beat your own dogs."

"Told you, I'm goin' to die."

If only that was true.

Wash couldn't help thinking it, and more. How easy it would be to clamp a hand over Mulholland's mouth and nostrils and fulfill the man's prophecy. No one would be the wiser, not his son or the camp meeting trustees or anyone else. Mulholland would be dead, as dead as Joe back at the Concho-Kiowa confluence, as dead as Wash had been inside all these years.

Wash would never know whether he would have acted on his dark thoughts, for a shadow swept over him and he found an unarmed Isom at his shoulder. The clergyman was huffing, but nowhere near the degree to which someone up in years would.

"Where's the others, Brother Isom?" asked Wash. "Mulholland here's goin' to need some help gettin' back."

"Aw, hell," said Mulholland, obviously not reluctant to swear around a minister. "Just give me a while and I'll get my legs back under me. Goin' down's got to be easier."

"What about your dogs? Sounds like they might be fixin' to tree somethin' up there."

"Ain't learned a thing about grizzlies, have you, Baker, goin' all the way back to that drive in eighty. Grizzlies don't tree. They'll lead a dog up high, just below the craggy tops, and go to circlin' a mountain. When they get tired, they back up to a big rock and set there facin' what's after them, slapping with those sledgehammer paws of theirs. Naw, you ain't learned a thing."

The bastard! Lying there smug when the muzzle of Wash's shotgun was only inches away!

"Ain't them bull terriers raisin' Cain!" Mulholland added.

Indeed, their barks and growls almost drowned out the bays of the bloodhounds. "They's fighters, if there ever was a fightin' dog. If you'd had a bull terrier on that drive, 'stead of that yellow mongrel, things might've turned out different."

Wash squeezed the grip of his shotgun and slid his fingers inside the trigger guard. Not another word! He wouldn't put up with another word about the could-haves and would-haves of that night from hell!

Wash was a twitch away from lifting the weapon when Mulholland, unsuspecting, rolled away, apparently focused on the slope above.

"Now where you suppose he's goin'?" mused Mulholland. "He don't even have a gun."

Wash checked. Isom was already twenty feet up the mountainside and pulling away, the split tail of his black cutaway coat flaring at the back of his matching wool trousers. Wash didn't know why anyone would wear his Sunday best on a hunt, but the preacher seemed dressed to bury someone.

Or to be buried.

Wash had recovered a little and began rising. "Brother Isom?" he called. "Better hold on and wait for somebody with a gun."

Isom continued his steady climb, loose rocks clinking under his black lace-up boots. Starting after the clergyman, Wash wished he hadn't rested so long; his muscles had tightened, making every step higher more difficult than ever.

"Get my age, you can't climb like you used to," Wash remarked. He was already out of breath again. "I'd appreciate you waitin' on me."

But the clergyman, stony in his silence, never slowed, and with every step up through the widespread ponderosas, the distance between the men grew.

"What you got in mind, Brother Isom?" Wash persisted. "That's a dangerous animal up there. Drop back down and tell me more about Elisha. A prophet, wasn't he?"

The only reply was the grinding of boots against talus.

Sleuth, who had stopped well shy of Mulholland, must have thought that Wash had been dispatched to punish, for the dog cowered as he neared. The hazel eyes below the folds of skin looked forlorn, and Wash realized how conflicted the hound must be. It was the nature of most dogs to want to please their respective owners, on whom they were dependent, and yet the very hand that fed Sleuth was also the hand that wielded a cruel whip.

Wash no longer cared if he angered Mulholland by interfering with his training. Reaching Sleuth, who now shrank more, he spoke in a gentle tone.

"Don't be scared. I'm not goin' to hurt you."

He patted the wrinkled head and felt a tremble, but as Wash went on past, the eyes followed him and the tail moved in a slight, tentative wag.

Mulholland must not have noticed the interplay, for Wash heard no objection. Regardless, something more important was developing, and as Wash struggled up after Isom, it shoved aside other concerns. Isom seemed in a dark place, a very dark place, and Wash didn't know where it was taking the clergyman. Wheezing, fighting a losing battle in trying to overtake the younger man, Wash continued to appeal, only to be met with silent rebuff that was more alarming than had Isom turned and sworn at him.

From ponderosa to ponderosa, Wash followed and reached the massive gateway of the unscalable gunsight canyon, which split a sheer cliff that must have soared five hundred feet. Looking up, he reeled as he took in the bold contrast of the jagged summit against the overhead sky. Drawn by glimpses of Isom and the barking of the dogs, he shunned the gulch and veered right, his shoulder sometimes scraping the face of the escarpment as he traced its folds across the windy heights.

It was a good thing that his course now spared him appreciable climbing, for the ascent had taken a terrible toll. He still labored for breath, and he felt so damned weak that it was all he could do to place one teetering foot after the other in dodging the spines of pitaya and hedgehog, pincushion and eagle claw.

Around an outcrop with a stand of prickly pear, he broke onto a recess—a small canyon, really. With the fading of day, it was thick with shadows except at a white-washed drainage that spilled around the far side of a huge boulder draped by a madrone's sleek, red limbs. The way ahead was hidden, but nothing could mute the vicious barks and growls that came from somewhere near a wind-whipped ponderosa that he could see through the madrone's dark-green foliage.

This wasn't a place to enter blindly. Maybe Mulholland was a blowhard prone to inciting unnecessary panic, but back at Rockpile, Wash had seen a track that had swallowed his size eleven boot. A killer lurked ahead, and common sense told Wash he would be taking a chance. But wisdom hadn't prevailed with Isom, and it couldn't now with a man obsessed with trying to correct a heinous mistake in any small way he might.

With the shotgun ready at his hip, Wash advanced, more afraid to live with the pain for another minute than to die.

As he rounded the boulder, there was no longer anything to muffle the bedlam of dogs on the attack. But strangely, Wash could hear only the mournful howl of a yellow mongrel as he had ridden away from a desolate grave at the Concho-Kiowa juncture. Could anything he might do in the coming moments bring greater rest for Joe, or for him? Wouldn't the two of them be just as dead, each in his own way?

In mid-step, an awful roar reverberated through the little canyon, shaking Wash out of introspection. Petrified, he peered up a rock-strewn drainage crisscrossed by creepers and lined with shrubby gooseberries and mountain snowberries. Twenty yards ahead, Isom stood to the right of the tall ponderosa, its bark weeping sap. The baying bloodhounds were beside him, and hounds and clergyman alike focused on the head of the little box canyon that ended another thirty yards away at blurs of color: the brindle of one bull terrier and the white of the other, moving against the dark brown of something much larger.

Backed up to a jumble of rock, just as Mulholland had described, the silver-tipped thing swung at its tormenters with lightning-fast paws that had broken a cow's neck. Dwarfed, the terriers seemed overmatched, but they were as quick as they were game, one dog distracting while the second terrier lunged and snapped.

Wash found his voice. "Get out of there, Brother Isom!"

Unquestionably, the bear had nowhere to go except back the way it had come—through the terriers and bloodhounds and Isom, if it so chose.

Wash called a second time, a third, but even as Isom continued to stand silent and motionless, the preacher seemed to fade into a striking darkness. He was no longer there, a troubled figure on an uncaring mountain, and neither was Wash, who abruptly was face to face with the gloom of a long-ago night—and out of it came a shadowy form that had lived all these years in Wash's nightmares.

Who's there!

How many, many times, through days of regret and nights of unbearable despondency, had Wash wished that he had done things differently when he had gotten no answer. He would have confronted the oncoming shadow like a man and not a coward, with his fingers outside the trigger guard, and accepted the consequences. At the time, he hadn't had the courage, but there was little need for courage now for a man who had so little for which to live.

The shadow from the here and now charged.

Even as Wash saw the onrushing bear in the light of day, the numbing memories kept him from reacting. But Isom was no less frozen as the bloodhounds turned and fled. The warning Wash wanted to shout died in his throat, and all he could do was watch the horrible end descend in flashes: the bursting power rippling the muscled hump and grizzled coat . . . the massive shoulders rolling from side to side . . . the slavering jaws yawning wide to crush.

A fiend that couldn't be stopped, the grizzly gave another thunderous bawl that rocked the canyon. Then the bull terriers were there, barking and leaping just before the great bear would have fallen upon Isom. The brindle latched onto the right ear. The white-and-black seized the throat. Growling savagely, both dogs held on, drawing the bear away from Isom even as their teeth were unable to pierce the tough hide.

The grizzly tried to shake the dogs loose, but the terriers' jaws had clamped tightly. The bear slung its head toward the brindle at its ear, the massive jaws snapping against air. Like a dog after its own tail, the grizzly wheeled completely around three times in fruitless chase as both terriers flew outward yet clung tenaciously.

But the bear was as determined as the dogs. Concentrating on the black-and-white at its throat, it stood upright, towering over nearby Isom, and used its paws to try to shove the terrier between its jaws. When the dog eluded all attempts, the grizzly roared and bolted down-canyon, evidently hoping to outrun what it couldn't dislodge.

Isom was in its path, and as the bear ran through him, the glancing blow scraped the brindle from its ear. Slammed against the pine, the preacher collapsed with the dog sprawled across him. Only now did Wash come out of his fog and shoulder the shotgun, but the bear closed on him quickly, the white-and-black terrier still fast at its neck.

Boom!

Wash squeezed both triggers simultaneously, but he must have been too careful to avoid shooting the dog, for mere gravel peppered the grizzly. Suddenly Wash could see only dark fur and four-inch claws and jaws ready to lacerate.

But the bear was intent on escaping, not mauling. The dangling terrier plowed into Wash's hip, a powerful blow that peeled the dog from the thick hide and threw Wash against the boulder. Stunned by the events but uninjured, Wash opened his break-action shotgun and ran out of the canyon a few steps. But before he could eject the empty shells and reload, the grizzly was out of range down the mountain with the bull terriers in pursuit. The hounds followed at a distance.

"Papa! You all right?"

On edge, Wash spun to the outcrop marking the mouth of the recess and found Grace rushing up with her .30-30 carbine. She was a crack shot—Wash had seen to that—but after what he had just lived through, he wished he had left her at the safety of the Rockpile.

"Ol' bear runnin' like a race horse!"

Tommy, with Sleuth at his side, was behind her, shading his eyes as he peered down the mountain. Trey had emerged as well, the setting sun glinting in his .30-40 Winchester.

"What happened here, Mr. Baker?" Trey asked.

Wash turned back to the little canyon. "We've got to see about Brother Isom. Bear run over him. Me too."

"Are you hurt, Papa?" pressed Grace, drawing his attention.

"Wish I'd sent you home with your mother. I don't want you anywhere near that bear."

Prudence told Wash that he shouldn't be either. Now that the desperate moments had passed, a debilitating weakness had come over him. His hand trembled as he reloaded, and even though there was no longer anything to fear in the canyon, his fingers were on the triggers as he edged around the shielding boulder.

Isom was sitting up against the ponderosa and shaking his head like a dazed ram. As Wash picked his way up the arroyo, he stumbled in the loose rocks more than he should have. When his daughter steadied him, he didn't know how to feel—old, he supposed, and tired out by all the years of punishing himself. He didn't feel any better when Trey and Tommy hurried past both of them, and by the time Wash reached the ponderosa, the younger Mulholland was down on a knee with his fingers on Isom's shoulder.

"Are you injured?" asked Trey. "There's a mark on your forehead. Did you hit the tree?"

When Isom lifted his head, he had a vacant look in his eyes.

"You sleepin', Preacher Isom?" asked Tommy. "Takin' you a nap with eyes open?"

Questions. Wash had plenty of his own for Isom, but that was a conversation better left for private.

With Trey's help, the clergyman came shakily to his feet and supported himself with a forearm against the ponderosa. He still hadn't spoken, but he was no less responsive than during the grueling ascent on foot with Wash.

"Ain't this somethin'!" exclaimed Tommy. "We's doin' it again like where Kiowa come in to the Concho!"

"Tommy . . ." cautioned Wash.

"That ol' bear and Little Trey, and Preacher Isom too, standin' in for his pappy!"

Wash didn't need a reminder of the dark moment, but excitement had taken hold of the slow-witted man.

"Not now, Tommy," Wash implored.

"Shotgun go off like hell a-poppin' and here I come runnin'!"

How far did Tommy intend to carry his comparison? Surely not to the point of—

"Found you holdin' ol' gun same way, Mr. Wash!"

"You've told enough."

But Tommy obviously didn't think so. "Only this time," he added, "you ain't up and shot your—"

Wash had spared even his own daughter the details of that night. Now they were being blurted out in the most callous of ways, and there was no way to stop it.

Abruptly Tommy was thwarted by the last person Wash would have expected.

"That's enough!" yelled Trey. He seized Tommy by the shoulders. "Some of us trying to forget that night!"

Taken aback, Wash didn't know what to make of the outburst, and in glancing around, it was clear that no one else did either. Tommy, with lips parted and eyes wide and round, went ashen. Isom's fog lifted a little, for he turned to the confrontation. Grace's confusion seemed greatest, for her gaze went from Wash to Trey and Tommy and back to Wash, as if she was beginning to piece together the things no one had ever spoken of to her.

Maybe Trey had intended to save Wash from a painful reminder, but that would have been out of character for any son of Ed Mulholland. Neither the father nor the son had ever shown any sensitivity about that night, much less expressed sympathy. More likely, Trey was trying to curry favor for courtship purposes. Either that, or . . .

Could something deeper be at play?

Regardless, the young man turned and withdrew toward the canyon head, his chin against his chest.

Wash's hand was down at his side, and when he felt something wet, he found Sleuth nudging his fingers. Panting and slobbering, the old dog begged for the gentle attention Wash had paid him back on the slope.

"Made yourself a friend."

Grace's subdued voice broke an uncomfortable silence.

"Better not let on around ol' man Mulholland," said Tommy. He turned and watched Trey continue to walk away. "Sure hope Little Trey ain't takin' after that mean ol' man."

As if Mulholland were there to see, Wash defiantly stroked the hound's wrinkled head. Then from somewhere down the mountain, the baying of the other hounds caught his ear.

"Sound of things, bear's headed back where we left the horses." Checking the sky, Wash found only the uppermost rock still in sunlight. "Time we get there, be too late to take in after him, short as these days are." He let out a weary breath. "I'm wore down, anyhow."

He felt Grace's hand on his arm.

"Let him go, Papa," she urged. "We'll make camp like we planned and just hunt deer tomorrow. The thing could have *killed* you and Brother Isom."

Wash heard the concern in her voice, and saw it in her creased forehead. But as memories deluged him again, he knew that nothing could kill two men who were already dead.

CHAPTER FIVE

I'll kill him, Papa. When I grow up, I'll kill him for you.

Out of yellow flames that lapped popping wood came a long-suppressed memory, and Grace scooted closer on her hip in search of warmth. There was a chill in the night air, having swept down from the concealed heights beyond the fire, but not so great a chill as to draw anyone else nearer the ring of blackened rocks. On the contrary, her father, on her right, as well as Tommy and Isom across from her, seemed content to sit at a modest distance and dodge the wafting smoke as they ate tiredly from airtights of beans and tomatoes. In the rearmost shadows on the lower right, Trey stood off to himself with his back turned, while under a pinyon pine thirty feet past her father, Mulholland rummaged through a saddlebag as Sleuth and the bull terriers waited hungrily.

Night had fallen across the slopes by the time Grace had reached the horses with her father, Tommy, and Isom. All the way from the upper reaches, Trey had lagged, ignoring her repeated summonses in the gathering dark. Fortunately, Mulholland's campfire had guided everyone down to this confined space on a forested shoulder of the mountain, although Trey had shown up late, well after the terriers had yielded the chase to the bloodhounds.

Now, as Grace scanned the big pinyons that hovered on all sides, the pines seemed like black figures standing in judgment, but against whom she didn't know.

The child she had been, for saying such a thing about Ed Mulholland?

Her father, for nurturing in his young daughter so vile a notion?

Or maybe it was Mulholland himself who deserved punishment for whatever his part had been in the long-ago tragedy.

Tommy had been on the verge of revealing much about that night, and the way Grace's father had lost all color, she feared that Tommy would have confirmed what she had long suspected. But there had to be more to be learned, and Trey's behavior only raised greater questions.

Snarling erupted as the terriers contended over jerky Mulholland had tossed on the ground. One strip had landed to the side, and the moment Sleuth moved hesitantly toward it, Mulholland's quirt cracked across the saggy hide.

"Get out of there!" Mulholland's whip flailed again. "Think I'm feedin' *you*? Be lucky if you get anything when them other dogs show up. You ain't worth killin'."

The firelight burned in the hound's eyes as he cowered in anticipation of more lashes. When no more came, Sleuth slunk away, as forlorn an animal as Grace had ever seen.

The flogging hadn't gone unnoticed by Wash, whose jaw muscles were working. As Sleuth crept toward the fire, the dog seemed to look at him. Wash's hand rested alongside his duck trousers, and Grace was surprised to see his crooked finger making a subtle "come here" gesture. The encouraged hound continued his submissive approach and soon lay next to him with frothy jowl across his thigh.

As the seconds dragged on and became a full minute, Grace tensed as though astride a green-broke horse sure to pitch at any moment. Then Mulholland turned to the fire and his face swelled.

"Baker! Thought I made myself clear. Ain't nobody to be

touchin' my dogs."

"I'm not touchin' him. He's touchin' me."

Mulholland came nearer. "Whatever you done ain't your business. Sleuth! Get the hell over here!"

The hound flinched and looked back at Mulholland.

"He's tremblin' all over," said Wash. "You can get more out of an animal—dog or horse either one—if you treat him with a little kindness instead of beatin' him."

"Who are you to be tellin' me how to treat my own stuff? Sleuth! Over here right now if you know what's good!"

All the way from the little canyon, Isom had brooded in near silence. Now, though, as he stared at his beans and twisted the can so that the firelight danced on it, he spoke up.

" 'I will punish the world for their evil, and the wicked for their iniquity.' " The quotation was all but lost in the crackle of the fire.

Again, Mulholland called Sleuth, and Grace saw her father's chest rise and fall.

"Better go," he told the dog.

When he slid his leg away and gave Sleuth a nudge, the animal crawled fearfully toward Mulholland's stern features.

"Poor ol' dog," Tommy said quietly. "Ain't right, just ain't right."

Grace hoped that Mulholland hadn't heard. Even if he was out of earshot, Tommy had a habit of talking increasingly louder when upset and was certain to stir up trouble if he dwelled on the matter. Just as Tommy started to say more, her father gained his attention.

"Say, Tommy, I need to get with you about somethin.' "

Rising, he went behind Grace and on around the fire so that Tommy had to turn his back to the dogs in order to face him.

"That blazed-face chestnut you broke for me last month." The older man sat down on Tommy's right, ensuring Tommy's

59

undivided focus. "Think he'll make a good cow pony?"

If anything could distract Tommy from the mistreatment of Sleuth, it was a discussion about horses. Soon the two of them were deep in conversation about the chestnut's bright eyes and other encouraging attributes.

But Tommy wasn't the only one whose conduct worried Grace. In the shadows, Trey remained as aloof to her as he was to everyone else. Ever since his flare-up in the little canyon, he hadn't said a word, although as she checked now and caught him staring, his lips were moving silently.

Trey turned away again, clearly unwilling to face her, and Grace swallowed her pride and started toward him to the snap of deadfall under her boots. The acrid smoke followed, but her eyes stung for an entirely different reason as she stopped behind him.

"You've never been this way before," she said.

His shoulders slumped. "What way is that?"

"You said you had some things on your mind. You never said what."

His voice stayed lifeless. "Nothing anybody can do anything about."

Grace didn't know what to do except speak from the heart.

"I . . . I'm worried what's come over you. Since this morning, what's . . ."

Trey wouldn't answer, and when Grace stepped around to face him, he pivoted away.

"Won't . . . Won't you even look at me?" she asked, her emotions raw. "Did I do something wrong? Tell me what I did, so . . . so I can make it right."

Grace tried again to face him, and in the moment before he denied her once more, she saw firelight in a glistening stream down his cheek.

"Trey?" she pleaded. "Talk to me. Please talk to me."

Despondence filled his voice. "Why . . . Why do you have to—"

The yelp of a dog cut him short, and Grace spun to see Mulholland's quirt fall across Sleuth's back.

"I'll teach you!" yelled the man. "Teach you or kill you, one!"

Trey, too, turned to the disturbance, and as more lashes popped, Grace distinguished his heartbreaking mutter about his father.

"Hid your quirt one time so you couldn't . . . Made it that much worse on me."

But for the moment, Grace couldn't concern herself with Trey, for Tommy went wild. He burst to his feet with flailing arms as his nostrils flared and the flickering light highlighted bulging veins in his temples.

"Ain't right, ain't right, ain't right!" he exclaimed. "Mean man ain't got no right treatin' poor ol' dog that away!"

Wash tried to calm him with quiet words and a hand on his arm, but Tommy slipped free and began to stalk around, his rant undeterred. Abruptly, Mulholland made it all about Wash.

"Baker, get your man to shut his mouth."

Now her father was on his feet and facing Mulholland. "You's the one can stop it. Just quit beatin' the dog."

"I'll damned well kill the thing if I've a mind. Why the hell you bring that man of yours, anyhow? Ain't good for nothin'."

"Tommy's got a right."

"Clabber-head dog's got more brains."

"Least, he's got horse sense," said Wash. "I'll take that and a tenderhearted streak any day over the likes of you."

When he stepped toward Mulholland, and Mulholland toward him, Grace didn't know how this would end. Then Isom was up as well, the ever-shifting smoke swirling about his legs.

"Balaam smote his ass three times and wanted to kill her, when it was his own self that needed chastising."

The clergyman's words were enough to stop the men's advance on one other.

"Don't you start up on me, preacher man," said Mulholland. "I got enough to put up with."

"We all need chastising," said Isom. "Some of us need to die."

"What's that mean? You sayin'—"

"Mean man! Mean man! Mean man!" Tommy still paced, wagging his head and talking to himself.

Mulholland slung a hand in his direction. "That any way for a growed man to act?"

"Tommy's different," interjected Wash. "Think you know that."

"Yeah, well, ain't no excuse. He—"

" 'Suffer little children,' " quoted Isom, " 'and forbid them not, to come unto me.' "

"What's that got to do with anything?" contended Mulholland.

"To receive a child in the Lord's name," said Isom, "is to receive the Lord."

Mulholland fell silent, and so did everyone else, even Tommy. As the uneasy hush persisted and each of the four men went about his own business, Grace placed her hand on Trey's shoulder.

"What you were asking, something about why I have to . . ."

But the door into Trey's soul had closed and he walked away, melding into a forest gloom as dark as Grace's own.

The swelling moon hung in the sky in constant reminder that it would soon be full.

Rosindo Mesa, who had just turned twelve, and his young sister Benita had been on the trail of *el oso plateado*, the silver bear, for ten days. From the grave in the Fronterizas of northern

Coahuila, they had followed the killer so Rosindo could free their *papá's* soul. With tracking skills passed down from father to son, Rosindo had traced the spoor through mountain defiles and across desolate reaches of Chihuahuan Desert ruled by spiny lechuguilla, ocotillo, and agave.

Watched only by twisted Spanish daggers, he and his sister had splashed the roan across the Rio Grande and clung to the trail through days of hunger and thirst under a relentless sun that seemed not to realize that mid-November was upon the land. At times, the spoor had vanished, but whenever Rosindo had closed his eyes, the dark *bulto* of their father had seemed to beckon and guide.

Now, in a high mountain valley between an isolated pile of boulders and a great rocky ridge that resembled the old *curandero's* gap-toothed smile, Rosindo lay staring up at the moon that dominated not only the night sky, but his thoughts.

Before the next full moon rises an hour in the sky, kill the silver bear or it will be too late!

The *curandero's* words had driven him all this way, but the time in which to do what Rosindo must was almost gone.

"I'm cold, Rosindo."

Benita lay on his right, and as he checked beyond her, he found that the fire had died down to embers that glowed and dimmed like the winking stars. He too was chilled, but he knew that to speak of it might only discourage her more. Sitting up, he tucked the woolen blanket around her shoulders and under her chin.

"You'll sleep warmer now, my sister."

Still, as he scooted closer, he could feel her shiver.

"When can we go back?" she asked. Her teeth chattered.

Rosindo knew what an ordeal the journey had been on a nine-year-old. "Things will be better when the sun comes up."

Benita sobbed. *"Home. I want to go home."*

Rosindo wouldn't remind her that they no longer had a home to which to return, only an empty adobe that would never again know the love of their *mamá* and *papá*.

"Just a little longer, Benita."

"When, Rosindo?" she pressed. "When?"

"I'll kill *el oso plateado* and we'll start back."

"Tomorrow?"

"Or the day after. Then we'll go back, I promise."

It was a promise Rosindo could make, for in two days the moon would rise full and their father's soul would either be free or doomed to wander forever.

"Kill the bear tomorrow!" pleaded Benita.

"If the saints smile on us," he acknowledged. "The trail was fresh yesterday. If we hear the dogs chase *el oso* again, we won't have to search for tracks."

"Maybe the bear's dead," she suggested. "We could start back!"

From high on the mountain at sunset, a gunshot had rolled across the valley, all right, but the dogs had continued to bay long after Rosindo had staked the roan and built a fire against the creeping chill.

"The bear's dead! The bear's dead!" Benita chanted hopefully.

But hope couldn't change what had happened in the Fronterizas, and it couldn't shape matters in this faraway place either.

"*El oso*'s alive, my sister. Even with the tracks of six riders in the trail, *el oso* still stalks the night."

"I want to go home. Let *them* kill *el oso*."

If only a solution were that easy. "I need to be the one, Benita. Remember? The *curandero* said I must do it."

Assuredly, the healer had made it clear, and with hunters ahead, the muchacho now had an added burden on his small shoulders. In less than two days, he must somehow get to *el oso plateado* first—or their *papá* could never reunite with them in Heaven.

CHAPTER SIX

"You won't be hunting the bear anymore, will you, Papa?"

Until Grace spoke over the campfire's hiss, Wash didn't know that she had come up behind him as he squatted on his heels before the charred fire ring. At daybreak, he had stoked the live coals and made coffee, only to stare into a steaming cup as black as a night that he could never escape.

"Sleep warm?" he asked, finding her over his shoulder.

His daughter drew the collar of her wool coat tighter under her chin. "There was frost on my tarp when I woke up."

"Mine too. First I've seen this year." Wash extended his cup. "Coffee? Hadn't touched it."

When Grace accepted and began to sip, Wash hoped she had ceased lobbying about his choice for the day's hunt. But she hadn't.

"Don't deer like to move around on frosty mornings?" she asked.

"Yeah," Wash acknowledged. "Not much interested in deer right now."

With no coffee in which to peer, Wash gazed at the fire and saw everything but the licking flames and the red embers that rose into the air and quickly died.

"Venison sure would taste good," she said.

"Guess I'm off my feed today."

Taking up a stick, Wash poked the fire and watched the yellow flames leap.

"You're not going, are you?" pressed his daughter. "After the bear, I mean."

The blaze held Wash's stare as wood popped and threw ashes against the blackened rocks.

"It's not worth it, Papa," Grace went on. "Let's get ready and find a deer."

From off toward the staked horses, Wash heard a loud, extended belch that would have rivaled the croak of the largest bullfrog back in Central Texas. Wash didn't have to turn to know that it was Mulholland, who had a crude habit of making a show of every gassy release even in mixed company.

Grace persisted in her appeal to Wash. "Stay with me today, why don't you? There's not anything to gain by going after that bear."

Mulholland belched again. "Got to disagree with you there, girl," he interjected. "Up in Colorado, they was a grizzly killed eight hundred cattle. Twenty years, they hunted him. If a thing like that ain't stopped, he'll keep eatin' till we's all on the poor farm."

Wash didn't care about the cattle, not right now, anyway.

"Papa," said Grace, ignoring Mulholland, "I don't want you to get hurt."

Mulholland couldn't stay out of the conversation. "Liable to, paradin' around with a shotgun like he is. Baker, you think buckshot's goin' to stop a grizzly? Hide's tough as can be, and they's a thick layer of fat underneath."

When Wash didn't say anything, and neither did Grace, Mulholland continued.

"Three ways to kill a grizzly, and they's all with somethin' like a .45-70, .30-40, or even a .30-30 maybe. You can shoot him in the throat, back of the ear, or through the shoulder. Anywhere else and he'll just get mad. He'll snap at the wound and snarl, and next thing you know, he's comin' right at you."

Wash had his reasons for carrying the shotgun, and nothing Mulholland could say would change his mind. Still, Wash found a deep breath, and he was still contemplating matters when he felt Grace's hand on his shoulder.

"It's too dangerous," she implored. "If Mama knew what nearly happened to you and Brother Isom, she'd say the same thing."

Again, Mulholland spoke up. "Soon's I feed my dogs, I'm takin' them up the mountain so's they can pick up the trail. Guess some men ain't cut out for it. Goin' up against a grizzly takes grit in your gizzard."

Wash had heard enough, from Mulholland and Grace both. His daughter, he could excuse, for he knew that she spoke out of love. But Mulholland . . .

"How much grit it take to beat a dog?" Wash challenged, without dignifying the man with even a glance.

Mulholland's spurs began to rattle and grow louder, but Wash continued to look at the fire.

"You got a real problem with that no 'count hound, ain't you," Mulholland snorted.

Only now did Wash stand and turn. Mulholland was almost to the fire ring, a flush across his puffed cheeks and on around to his ears.

"No," said Wash, taking a step toward him. "I got a problem with you."

Until now, the others in camp had tended to their own matters. When Wash had built up the fire, he had seen a yawning Tommy sit up in his blankets, stretch, and run fingers through his tangled hair before lying back. At a neatly coiled bedroll, Isom had stood with head bowed as if in reflection or prayer. Trey had seemed disinterested in the fire, even in the chill, and Wash had glimpsed him stirring in seclusion in the pinyons.

Wash didn't know what any of the three were doing now, but

Grace wasn't standing idly. Abruptly she was between Mulholland and him.

"What's the matter, Baker?" asked Mulholland. "Hidin' behind a damned girl?"

Wash was ready to tear him apart, and he might have if a voice hadn't come from beyond the fire.

"Father! Take your hat off to Miss Grace and tell her you're sorry."

Checking, Wash saw Trey emerging from the pinyons.

"What the hell for?" Mulholland demanded of his son.

"For swearing in front of her. You just did it again."

"Since when you tell me what to do? I'm your daddy, boy."

"Haven't been a boy for ten years. Even when I was, I knew when you did right with a quirt and when you did wrong."

Mulholland, his face redder than ever, said something under his breath. *Damned cur,* Wash thought it was. But there was no mistaking what the man said next as he whirled on Grace.

"See what you stirred up, steppin' in where it ain't your place? All you Bakers is alike. Both of you can . . ."

Say it! Wash cried silently. *Tell my girl she can go to hell, and I'll end things right here!*

But Mulholland's voice trailed away and he retreated toward his saddlebags.

Wash could tell that his daughter wanted to speak with Trey, for her eyes lighted up and she took a half step in his direction. But Trey never looked at her, proceeding instead to withdraw back into the pinyons and leave Grace to study his unaware father across the camp.

The day before, Wash would have been pleased to see Trey ignore his daughter. But after watching him demand propriety in her presence, Wash wondered if there was more to the young man than he had given him credit for.

The elder Mulholland, though, was exactly the man Wash

69

knew him to be, and as Wash stared at him through the bitter smoke—a piercing stare that Grace uncharacteristically seemed to share—a whisper long-buried in memory came to him as clearly as if spoken now.

I'll kill him, Papa. When I grow up, I'll kill him for you.

With a start, Wash spun to Grace, for he realized that he had heard the words not in memory, but on his daughter's lips this very moment.

Snow dust swirled in the air.

For up-and-down miles by horse toward the heart of the mountains, Wash had been unable to see the ominous north sky behind the pinyons, junipers, and gray oaks. It had stayed hidden even as the norther had struck with a fury, whistling through the stirring limbs and crawling down his collar despite his neckerchief. Then his horse had climbed out of the trees and Wash had looked back, finding a blue-black bruise covering half the sky—a harbinger of freezing rain that soon had iced the stems of Indian paintbrush and purple dalea that grew among the slope's glazed rocks.

Now, as the Appaloosa threaded its way along a narrow shelf under an impassable rise on the right, an updraft lifted powdery snow out of a dramatic canyon that fell away sharply on the opposite side. Wash's left boot, secure in a stirrup as he looked, seemed to ride free in the air, tracing an eagle's path against a parallel canyon five hundred feet below.

This wasn't a place for a horse to stumble, or else Wash's penance for so many things would be over in a hurry.

I'll kill him, Papa.

For all these years, Wash had buried the memory of kneeling beside his six-year-old daughter and helping her capture the gray oak's bark in the sights of a cocked revolver. He had guided her tiny index finger through the trigger guard and slipped his own over hers, ready to apply the pressure that would drive the firing pin against the cartridge. To their shared efforts, the Colt Single Action Army had roared again and again, and he had prefaced every shot with words of vengeance that Grace finally had appropriated for herself.

When I grow up, I'll kill Ed Mulholland for you.

Now, as the memories raged like the biting wind, Wash was stunned that any father could instill so vile a thing in an impressionable young girl. No matter his feelings about Mulholland, it had been abuse of the worse kind, beyond excuse or forgiveness, and Grace had carried it with her from childhood. To what end, Wash was terrified to contemplate.

All the way from last night's camp, he had wanted to broach the matter with her, but he hadn't known what to say. He still didn't know. The only thing of which he was certain was that if there was a hell, his place in it was more assured than ever.

For half an hour, Wash had been out of earshot of the hounds. Their last bays, faint in the distance, had been along this bearing, and all he could do was ride on and hope to hear their cries again. The sough of the norther drowned out so much, but the rattle of the saddle and grind of the hoofs were in his control, and he held the Appaloosa and listened for what must have been minutes.

Wash couldn't hear the hounds, but from behind came the rhythmic crunch of hoofs against icy rock. The party had stayed bunched until the hounds had picked up the trail, and as soon as the dogs had raced away in full cry, Wash had forged to the front. With every mile, he had stretched his lead, but when he looked back now, he saw a bay horse approaching with its rider. The way Isom abruptly drew rein while the animal was still thirty feet away led Wash to believe that the clergyman had overtaken him without realizing it.

Too many things vied for Wash's thoughts. But in reflection it seemed that the clergyman had avoided him since the grizzly encounter. With the two men finally alone, the troubling questions were a powerful presence again.

"Bring your horse on up here, Brother Isom," Wash said over the wind.

At first, Isom did nothing. Then Wash motioned, and the clergyman brought the bay closer. Soon Isom was near enough for Wash to speak without shouting.

"It's miserable out here. You's not even huntin'. If this ever *was* fun, it's sure not now. How come you don't go on back home?"

Isom turned his face into the teeth of the storm and stared as the snow dust mottled his steel-wire spectacles and goatee.

"It won't quit, Brother Baker. It won't ever stop."

"A blue whizzer of a norther, all right."

"He keeps crying and crying and . . ."

Not again, thought Wash.

"He killed my Lela," continued Isom, "and he keeps crying and crying and—"

"All you's hearin' is the wind, like before," interrupted Wash. "Why don't you start on back home. Warmin' by the fireplace's got to be better than this."

He didn't think it possible for a face so flushed to go ashen, but Isom's did. Abruptly the preacher seemed in another place, another time.

"Yes . . . The fire . . . I was sitting there staring at it."

"Sure would feel good right now," said Wash.

But that wasn't the memory that the clergyman was reliving.

"Lela was gone, but I could see her in the fire. Lela . . . Lela . . . What can I do? The child's crying . . . always crying . . . Make him stop . . . make him stop . . ."

Wash had intended to probe Isom about confronting the bear, but he thought better of it. The clergyman was in no condition to look inside himself.

"You'd feel better if you was in out of all of this," said Wash. "Weather like this can drag a man down lots of ways."

"To perdition," muttered Isom, bowing his head. "Down to hellfire itself."

From the resignation in his voice to the quivering chin and drooping shoulders, the clergyman was the portrait of despair.

"Don't like the way you's soundin', Brother Isom. Buck up, or you'll get yourself in awful shape."

But there seemed no consoling him, and as Wash struggled with how to respond, he was glad to see the other riders approach single-file, the only means possible on the narrow shelf. In the lead was Mulholland, his red face as swollen in anger as ever.

"What's this pow-wow you got goin' on?" he demanded.

Wash merely looked at him.

"Can't get after my hounds." Mulholland withdrew a flask from his coat and took a nip. "The two of you's blockin' the way."

Tommy, on his dapple gray, was directly behind Mulholland. "Can't hear Sleuth no more, the poor ol' dog."

"None of them's made a peep for a while now," said Wash. He glanced over the Appaloosa's ears at the ongoing shelf. "Last I could tell, they was up in this direction somewhere. Wonder if they lost the trail."

Mulholland brushed the snow from his brow. "That sorry ol' hound you's so fond of couldn't find his nose on the end of his face."

"Good ol' dog, Sleuth is," defended Tommy.

Undeterred, Mulholland continued. "Them other hounds is top-notch. But grizzlies is smart. Only animal they is that'll hide its own trail. He'll double back and jump here to there, usin' rocks and logs to keep from layin' down his spoor. You'll think he's ahead, and first thing you know, he's stalkin' you from behind."

Mulholland paused, breathless at this altitude. Maybe, too, he waited for someone to compliment his knowledge of grizzlies. If so, no one cared to.

"Baker," he said, "you got to get out of my way."

Clearly, Mulholland knew that the sudden drop on one side and the sharp rise on the other made that impossible at this point. Still, there was no benefit to sitting on a horse here and freezing, so Wash urged the Appaloosa ahead along the shelf.

A hundred yards farther, a place opened up just wide enough to turn a pair of horses out to the side.

"Pull out here with me, Brother Isom," said Wash. "Mulholland's in a big hurry."

Letting the latter man and his bull terriers brush by, Wash was glad to get rid of the worthless so-and-so. Wash distanced himself even more by allowing Isom, Tommy, and Trey to precede him. As his daughter's roan came abreast, Wash held out his arm.

"Hold your horse here a minute." He watched the hindquarters of Trey's dun recede. "Wait till he's out of hearin'."

With the separation growing and the wind gusting, Wash gathered his courage and turned to Grace, remembering her as a six-year-old.

"Some things I got to talk to you about."

Grace inclined her head and slumped in the saddle. "Mama said I better tell you before you noticed."

Clearly, the two of them were talking about different things.

His daughter continued. "She said you'd have a hissy fit quick as you found out."

"Found out what?" Wash would leave to her the responsibility of saying it.

Grace looked up tentatively. "Me and . . . Trey."

Wash breathed sharply. Even though he had known what she would say, the words stung. "You and that Mulholland boy."

"Papa, he can't help who his father is."

Wash looked away. Of course, she was right, but he couldn't forget what he had always heard. *Blood will tell.*

"You can always figure the kind of calves you'll get by the kind of bull you run," he said. He faced her again. "A *Mulholland*. Thought my own daughter would have more sense."

Grace hung her head once more, but he could still see the sadness in the drooping corners of her mouth. He didn't like upsetting her. He had been a bad enough father already, to both his children.

"You don't have to worry, Papa," she said with a half sob. "I don't think he wants anything to do with me anymore."

"Oh?"

"He was all right yesterday morning. Then he went to acting peculiar soon as the grizzly talk started up."

The grizzly. For Wash, it had stirred memories of another silver-tipped bear. Strangely, he had never considered the impact the tragedy on the Concho might have had on Trey, who had been pals with Wash's son. Was it possible that Trey carried trauma from watching Joe get shot and killed at his very side?

And by Grace's own father, no less.

"He won't even look at me anymore," added Grace.

Wash stared down at his saddle horn. "For the best, I guess." But when he heard another stifled sob, he looked at her with compassion. "I thought he did good, the way he stood up for you to Mulholland. The old devil's been the cause of a lot of grief."

"Papa, you hadn't ever told me. Mama won't neither."

"Told you what?"

"How Joe died. Why you blame Ed Mulholland."

Wash found himself focusing on the scarred stock of his

shotgun, angling up in the scabbard under his leg.

"Some things, it's better never to talk about."

"Papa, you . . . you shot him, didn't you. By accident."

The shotgun went blurry. But it would always be there, reminding, torturing, punishing, even in a near-blizzard as Wash perched on a cliff with eternity staring up at him.

"I . . ." His voice wouldn't work. "With a grizzly around, I give orders for ever'body to stay put. So black you couldn't see your own hand 'less it lightninged. Plenty of it, too, like hell goin' off. If anybody had business about—switchin' out ridin' guard or what-have-you—they was to answer back if somebody challenged them.

"We was all on edge, expectin' somethin' to bust out of the dark, get us while we was sleepin'. Mulholland's doin', ever' bit of it. We'd seen that beef with its neck broke, half-eaten, and he pointed out all the tracks and said it was a grizzly. 'A man-killer,' he kept sayin'. 'If you see somethin' comin' at you in the dark, shoot or you's good as dead.'

"Joe and Trey had their bed there together by the wagon with the rest of us. What little sleep I was gettin', I was holdin' on to my shotgun. I could just imagine that bear grabbin' Joe out of his bedroll and draggin' him off in the dark.

"I guess I'd dozed off, when a clap of thunder woke me up. Heard somethin' stirring out behind the wagon, so I got up, boots already on. Went right by where the boys was sleepin', but it was so dark I couldn't even see their tarp on the ground.

"I tripped on the wagon tongue when I went around. Both barrels would've gone off if I'd've had them cocked. Not a night goes by that I don't wish they'd've did it.

"Out back of the wagon, I heard somethin' comin' straight at me, so I thumbed back the hammers. 'Who's there!' I hollered, and about that time come a flash of lightnin' and I saw it, just a shadow. I yelled again, 'Who's there!' and nobody would answer

76

me. All I could hear was Mulholland back at the tracks. *'Man-killer! See somethin' comin' in the dark, shoot it! You got to shoot it!'*

"Joe and Mulholland's son, it was them. My boy! I killed my own boy!"

Wash had never wept in front of Grace, or Emma either. But when he buried his face in a hand, he felt wetness against his fingers.

"I-I'm sorry, Papa." He heard a lot of emotion in Grace's voice. "I'm sorry I made you tell me."

"Never knew what the two of them was doin' out there," Wash managed. "Joe was dead and couldn't tell me, and Trey just had a vacant look in his eyes the rest of the trip. I figured he blocked it all out, but hearin' what you told me, I wonder."

"You think," asked Grace, "with the bear and all, he's—?"

"Hadn't been much of a father, have I," Wash interrupted. "First Joe, and then the way I've tried to make you into him your whole life. Even worse, the way I brought you up to where I put somethin' awful in the head of a little girl that didn't know any better. I—"

His soul bared, Wash turned away, not wanting her to see him like this. Lifting his gaze to the ongoing ledge, he caught movement eighty yards ahead where a pair of riders hugged the mountainside. Someone was waving, a frantic summons, and the best he could tell, it was Tommy.

"Somethin' goin' on up there," said Wash, turning his horse along the shelf.

He was aware that his daughter followed. He still had a lot to talk over with her and find out—the extent of the hatred and vengeance he had conveyed that she still carried inside—but he wasn't sorry that events ahead had diverted their attention. He had already probed the depths of his self-worth deeper than ever before, and he didn't think he could bear anymore right now.

CHAPTER SEVEN

"Mr. Wash! He done went after it, Mr. Wash! Little Trey done went after Mr. Grizzly!"

The frigid wind had been alive with Tommy's excited cry long before Wash drew rein before the lone rider and distinguished the words. Tommy held his dapple gray at the head of a narrow ravine—a chute, really—that fell away on the left toward the depths five hundred feet below. Only yards wide, the ravine eventually disappeared over the contour of the mountain, and its snow-dusted course was scarred by recent passage that had exposed the underlying soil and rubble.

"You sayin' Trey went down here?" asked Wash. "How come?"

"I seen it first, Mr. Wash! I says, 'Look yonder! It's Mr. Grizzly swingin' his head side to side goin' down through that deep ol' canyon!' Little Trey don't say a thing. Soon as he looks, he turns his horse down this gully here."

"Papa, that's awfully steep." From behind came Grace's concerned words.

"Little Trey sure a good rider," reassured Tommy. "Horse of his sittin' back on his haunches and slidin', front feet keepin' balance. Can't hear it thunder in this ol' wind, but might've heard him holler after he gone out of sight."

"Papa . . ." The unease in Grace's voice grew.

Wash peered down the ravine and cupped a hand around his mouth. In all the years since the cattle drive, he didn't think he had ever addressed Ed Mulholland's son directly, and it felt unnatural doing so now. For Grace's sake, he called out, but he couldn't bring himself to include Trey's name.

"You all right down there?"

The only answer was the rush of the wind.

Wash shouted again, and this time Grace joined him. When no response came, Wash stepped off his horse.

"Might be close to the bottom already," he said. "I'll drop down and see about him."

"Want me to hold ol' Appaloosy, Mr. Wash?" asked Tommy.

"I'll go ahead and lead him down. If it's passable, I'll need him for that bear. With this bad knee, I don't care to climb back up unless I got to."

With the cold, Wash's legs were stiff as he led the horse by the reins into the shallow ravine. He couldn't afford to stay in front and chance being run over, so upon reaching the bed he let the animal come abreast on the left. Side-by-side, they started down the slope, the Appaloosa bumping him as it descended almost as Tommy had described: virtually resting on its haunches and sliding while it maintained balance with its forefeet.

The banks on either side rose higher, for Wash abruptly saw them from the perspective of a man who couldn't stand. To be sure, he was in a barely controlled skid on hips or back as his boots plowed the snow in front.

He quickly grew alarmed. There was no way to slow, much less stop, even by slapping his free arm out to the side, and the way ahead stayed hidden in the chute's contour. For all he knew, he could be moments from a sheer cliff, and he asked himself why he was risking his life for a Mulholland.

But Wash knew already. He had failed not only his son, but his daughter as well, and he had to do whatever he could to make it up to her.

Helpless, he barreled on, drawn blindly down the undulating

slope through a spray of snow as the Appaloosa's stirrup bounced and battered him. Then rock bit into his back and there was nothing but air under his boots, and with a cry that must have echoed what Tommy had heard from Trey, he plunged toward the unseen.

Horsehide and saddle leather fell with him. From eight feet below, a white ledge flew up at an angle with punishing force. Suddenly the sky and mountain were mere glimpses, spinning before Wash as he tumbled toward a scrub pinyon at a second pour-off fifteen feet from the first. A dun horse was already there, and the Appaloosa must have struck it a glancing blow, for the dun stumbled closer to an icy brink draped by its reins.

God Almighty.

Wash came to rest all too near a drop that might not end for hundreds of feet. Addled as he lay prone, he took a moment to get his bearings. Beside him, the Appaloosa again jostled the dun in struggling up, and through two sets of stirring forelegs Wash saw the dun's taut reins slip farther over the edge.

What in the hell . . .

At once, full awareness returned. Something heavy clung to those reins, someone who hung out of sight—and Wash spoke his name for the first time in all these years.

"Trey!"

Scrambling to the edge and peering over, Wash traced the reins down to a limp form, conspicuous against the snow-shrouded greenery far below in the canyon bottom. Trey's head had fallen to the side, and all that spared him from a sleep as deep as Joe's were leather reins twisted around his extended arm.

"I'm here!" shouted Wash. "Hold on!"

But Trey gave no indication that he was alive, much less understood.

Drawing back, Wash frantically searched for something—for

anything. To his right, the ledge threaded onward, narrowing to only a few feet. Under the bellies of the two horses on his left, he could see the exposed base of the gnarly pinyon, which seemed to grow out of solid rock only inches from the cliff. He had no good choices, but he couldn't go back and tell Grace that he had done nothing while Trey had fallen to his death.

Edging under the Appaloosa and then the dun, Wash slithered past the nervous hoofs and reached the small pinyon. Blanketed with white, the pine was barely more than shrub-high, and when he seized it, a shower of snow fell from its limbs. It was a hell of a thing, relying on an unstable runt of a tree to keep him alive, but Wash held to it with one hand and leaned dangerously far over the cliff's edge.

Trey, suspended against the rock wall, was subject not only to wind, but to the dun's every movement. Like an executed man in a noose, he dangled, his boot heels clicking together as the reins sawed into the rim's edge. The leather's hold on his arm was fragile, threatening to slip at any moment, and as Wash reached for the young man's wrist and grazed it, the pinyon creaked and bent in warning.

Terrified, Wash withdrew to the safety of the ledge. As his heart hammered, he weighed everything—the certainty of Trey's death, the inadequacy of the pinyon, the long drop into forever if he acted foolishly. But most of all, Wash considered his love for Grace, and once more he sprawled head down over the cliff as wind-driven snow half blinded him.

Even as Wash clutched Trey's wrist, he knew it wouldn't be enough. He was a sixty-year-old man, hanging upside down over a cliff, and he didn't have the leverage or strength to draw up one hundred sixty pounds of dead weight.

"Trey! Trey Mulholland!"

The head moved.

"Up here!" Wash cried. "Look at me! Open your eyes and look!"

Trey shook his head as if trying to clear the cobwebs.

"You got to help!" added Wash. "You hear me?"

When Trey raised his chin and revealed a cut above his brow, his blue eyes seemed somewhere else.

"You got to help!" Wash repeated. "You got to climb up!"

Trey's eyes were still glassy, but his free hand began to claw at the rock face. When his fingers clamped Wash's wrist, the pinyon screeched and sagged even more ominously. But Wash never wavered, pulling grimly as he stared down at a face that seemed to take on the features of Grace more than Trey.

Inch by inch, Wash's burden ascended, the boots kicking against the wall and finding toe-holds. When Trey planted a forearm across the ledge, it seemed almost certain that they would get out of this alive—and then came a *crack!* and the pinyon in Wash's grip gave way to his cry.

Dirt and rock dropped with him, the force wrenching his hand from Trey's wrist. But Wash slipped only a foot or so, the pinyon holding again even though partly unrooted. His legs were still mostly on the ledge, but he would have plunged headfirst if hadn't planted his free arm against the wall.

For seconds or an hour, he clung there, head down, afraid to move for fear of losing his tenuous balance, and yet knowing he had to. Then something seized his leg and his belt, and little by little the rock face moved until he was once more on the ledge.

He lay on his side, his lungs heaving. He didn't think he would ever catch his breath, or muster the strength to lift his cheek from the icy rock. When he eventually rolled over, he was between the two horses, and a hovering Trey blotted out the sky.

"You's bleedin'," said Wash. "Over your eye."

Not only did a thin stream of red run down the stubbly face, but there still didn't seem to be anyone home in Trey's eyes.

"You got knocked sky-western crooked," added Wash, sitting up. "You need to stop the bleedin'."

Trey didn't seem to grasp what he was saying, and Wash untied his neckerchief and passed it into the young man's hand.

"Hold it above your eye," said Wash. "The left one."

Wash had to repeat it, but Trey complied, applying direct pressure as the wind whipped the neckerchief's corners.

"Not sure I'd be here if you hadn't helped me," said Wash.

Dragging himself up alongside Trey by means of a stirrup leather, he steadied himself against first one horse and then the other and assessed their predicament. Taking the horses back up the gully was out of the question, for the animals could never climb the initial pour-off. Over the dun's snow-powdered saddle, the way was just as impassable, but beyond the Appaloosa, Wash again noted the tapering shelf continuing along the same bearing they had followed from higher on the mountain.

He pointed to it, but he was concerned by how the shelf hugged a drop as deadly as the pour-off beside the pinyon.

"Looks like the only chance we got of gettin' the horses out. Scary venture, though. Awful scary."

"Dare you," Trey abruptly whispered.

Wash turned, not sure that he had heard correctly. "What?"

"Dare you," said Trey, this time unmistakably. "I dare you, Joe."

Wash could only stare into eyes as glazed as ever.

CHAPTER EIGHT

"I . . . I don't . . . just can't . . ."

Whatever Trey wanted to say, the words wouldn't come.

Through the frozen canyon bottom they rode, the snow-laden limbs of pinyons and junipers hovering on either side as white whorls rose from the hoofs. Up on the mountain, Wash had sat him down until his eyes had cleared. Even so, Trey had stayed silent as they had carefully traversed the tapering shelf and reached a manageable slope that had allowed them to descend. Now as they traced the great bear's tracks in the snow, Wash had the nose of his Appaloosa even with the young man's left stirrup.

"I can't understand." Trey finally achieved a coherent sentence.

"Understand what?"

"You taking such a chance. Helping me."

Even as Wash studied the blood-soaked bandana around the rider's forehead, Trey wouldn't look at him.

"Didn't think you had wits enough on that cliff to know what I was doin'," said Wash.

"I was there and I wasn't. Part of the time it was like I was watching."

"Scary as it was, might've been better that way."

"You could've left me," said Trey, "let what was going to happen, happen. Maybe it would've been fitting, even now."

"What's *that* mean?"

84

Trey shrugged. "You almost killed yourself helping me. Of all people, me."

"Somebody hangin' from a cliff by his reins, nobody else around. What kind of man would I be if I didn't?"

Trey held his horse, and when Wash did so as well, the two men faced one another.

"Better than me," said Trey. "Whether you helped me or not, you'd be a better man than me."

Wash frowned. "You's makin' about as much sense as you did on the ledge."

"Sir?"

"You was talkin' crazy. Even said somethin' about Joe."

The color drained from Trey's face and his chin fell against his chest. "Joe . . ."

Wash didn't think a single word could carry so much anguish, and it summoned up his own turmoil.

"My friend," Trey continued. "The best I ever had."

Was that a bead that rolled down his cheek?

"I . . . I know y'all was pals," acknowledged Wash. "Even before the drive."

"Never had a brother, neither one of us." Trey's words came slowly, painfully. "I guess I thought of him that way. Him too, I imagine, seeing we were the same age. Far back as I can remember, we were always getting in a fix. One time it'd be me the cause of it, and next time it'd be him. No matter, it always took both of us to get us out. Somehow we always did, till . . ."

The young man turned away, and his shoulders began to quake.

Abruptly there was no snow, no crowding slopes, no howl of wind. For Wash, there was only night, and the recoil of a shotgun to a muzzle flash that broke the dark.

"I . . . I've had lots of trouble in my time," Wash managed, his voice hoarse. "But nothin' ever troubled me like this."

Trey didn't seem capable of saying more, and Wash looked down, his saddle horn fuzzy and his eyes burning. He had never realized how close the boys had been. He was even more surprised by the emotion Trey showed. All these years later, Trey was distraught over something about which Wash would never have believed that the son of Ed Mulholland had ever given a second thought.

"I'd give my whole life, that moment forward, for it not to have happened," said Wash.

When he lifted his head, Trey was looking at him, the blue eyes glistening.

"I'm sorry, Mr. Baker." Trey's chin quivered. *God help me, I'm sorry!*

It almost seemed an expression of guilt rather than sympathy, and Wash was bewildered. "Son, I . . ."

Wash didn't know what to say. In all these years, he had never had even a commonplace exchange with Trey, and now the young man laid bare, in puzzling terms, emotions that men rarely showed.

But maybe Trey was still addled. Maybe he would have been embarrassed to realize what he was saying. Or maybe, considering what Grace had related, the appearance of the grizzly had summoned up issues unresolved since that night on the Concho.

They rode on, the silence broken only by the roar of a shotgun a lifetime ago.

Thirty minutes passed, the horses sinking to the fetlocks in snow as Wash leaned over between the animals and traced the grizzly's fading tracks. He had much on his mind—people, places, and events, all jumbled together—and abruptly his own voice caught him unawares.

"My girl thinks a lot of you."

"Sir?"

Wash looked up, realizing what he had said. "I didn't know

nothin' about y'all. Wasn't till yesterday I started catchin' on."

"Miss Grace . . ." Trey glanced down. "She . . . She's a fine girl."

"Guess she was afraid to say somethin' to me, seein' how you's a Mul—"

This time, Wash curbed his tongue. There was no benefit to badmouthing a man to his son.

"I appreciate you takin' up for her this mornin'," Wash added. "Showed me somethin'."

"Father had no right to say what he did. Miss Grace deserves better." Trey's shoulders bent and he sank in the saddle. "She deserves better than me too."

Again, Wash was unsure how to respond. "She's all mixed up right now. Upset. Don't like seein' her that way."

"Upset?"

"Guess y'all had a spat."

For several paces of the horses, the young man didn't say anything, and neither did Wash. When Wash did say more—"It's between y'all, anyhow"—Trey talked over him. "I wouldn't hurt her for . . ."

Wash went quiet, yielding.

". . . for the world," completed Trey. "I just can't deal with it right now."

Wash wasn't going to press the issue. After all, he was pleased, in a way, that there was a rift between his daughter and this son of Ed Mulholland. But somehow he didn't find it satisfying.

As they rode on, the piercing wind grew thicker with snow that eddied around the Appaloosa's ears and collected on Wash's thighs. Two hundred feet high on the left, above timber and an imposing colonnade of rock, the snow blew in over the crest like a ghostly army, lurching and swaying. As Wash looked up, it seemed to descend like a pall, blinding and demoralizing, and when he checked the ground between the horses again, there was no longer even the suggestion of a trail.

"Hold on," he said, drawing rein. "Tracks has gone off another way. Either that, or they're buried up."

Truth be told, with his chaotic thoughts, Wash had lost concentration some time ago. He supposed Trey had as well, for when Wash joined him in looking back, only the spoor of their horses marked the snow as far as he could see.

Wash straightened in the saddle. "You got young eyes," he said, studying the snow ahead. "See any sign?"

Abruptly Trey slid his .30-40 Winchester out of its saddle scabbard. "I think we should be on guard, Mr. Baker."

Wash turned with Trey to the brush left and right.

"Hear somethin'?" Wash asked.

Trey stayed watchful as he levered a cartridge into the Winchester's chamber with a *click-click*.

"I'm not sure. Just a feeling, I guess. Father said a grizzly's smart."

"He says lots of things," Wash said doubtfully.

"A grizzly," continued Trey, "can circle back and come up behind you. Maybe he's just curious. Or maybe you think you're hunting him when he's really hunting you."

Wash didn't like the sound of that, and he reached alongside the saddle horn for the shotgun stock protruding from its boot. His head was down for only a moment—a moment of lax vigilance that caught him unprepared when his Appaloosa shied.

"Look out!" cried Trey.

The Appaloosa spun with Wash at the same instant, and all his years of riding couldn't stop the inevitable. The saddle slid away, the cantle scraping his leg, and then sky and horsehide and snow flashed and wheeled. Suddenly Wash's shoulders were on the ground, his boot still in the stirrup. A powerful force jerked his extended leg, and he realized that the bolting animal dragged him by his heel.

For awful seconds he bounced and twisted, and when his foot came free, something dark blotted out the sky. He glimpsed silver-tipped fur as he sprawled, and through the leather upper of his boot he felt the rake of lethal claws. Then a rifle cracked, and even before the report rolled through the canyon, he heard jaws snap like the sharp spring of a steel trap. With a roar of pain, the thing above him withdrew, and Wash never got a good look before the grizzly vanished into the timber under the great rock columns.

"Mr. Baker!"

Checking, Wash saw Trey on guard with the rifle as he brought his horse closer. The young man's wide, blue eyes, focused beyond Wash, were alert for any other threat that might emerge.

"Lord A'mighty," said Wash, with a glance toward the brush. Now that it was over, a great weakness came over him. "Bear must've come out of nowhere. Don't know what would've happened if you hadn't shot."

Trey maintained his vigilance. "Wasn't me."

"Wasn't—?" Wash gave a quick look around.

"Report came from up there." Trey pointed with the carbine barrel to the rim above the connected towers of rock. "From where I was, I couldn't get a shot off for fear of hitting you. Whoever fired must have been true to the mark. The bear snapped its jaws back along its hip."

"Yeah, I heard it."

"It didn't have any troubling running, though," said Trey. "Father says you have to shoot one dead on, or the lead will just graze the fat."

Wash didn't like hearing confirmation that Mulholland may have known what he was talking about, even in this one instance.

"Some of our bunch must have worked their way around," Wash observed, using the dangling coil of Trey's catch-rope to pull himself up. His trouser leg was hiked up over his boot, thereby allowing the cold to seep through, and when he took a moment to address it, he was shaken to find the leather upper sliced as if by a sharp knife.

Wash called Trey's attention to it. "That's how close I come to havin' claws gut me."

"Should've been me," the young man said quietly. "Both times—me."

"What?"

Trey seemed taken by surprise by what he had blurted, for he squinted and his mouth went slightly ajar. Just as quickly, he masked his reaction and yielded the stirrup.

"Step up and we'll go look for your horse, Mr. Baker."

With Trey's help, Wash swung up into the saddle behind him. But with every pace of the dun, Wash tried to understand what troubled this young man who still considered Joe his best friend.

Two hundred feet below, through spirit wisps of driven snow, Rosindo saw the great silver bear flinch as he squeezed the trigger.

But *el oso plateado* didn't fall. As Rosindo rocked to the rifle's recoil and the blast rolled through the canyon, the bear wheeled from the defenseless man and fled into the near-side timber.

From this partly wooded ridge, Rosindo and Benita had stealthily paralleled the six riders traversing the far mountain slope. The party had split, but from on high, the muchacho and his sister had continued to skirt the course of the horsemen who had descended. From beyond rifle range, Rosindo had watched the bear precede the two down-canyon, where the animal eventually had veered into the pinyons and junipers and waited for the hunters to pass.

Guided by flashes of *el oso plateado* through white-coated limbs, Rosindo had kept pace on his roan as the bear had come up behind the unaware men. He had seen how his father had died, so when the riders had stopped and the grizzly had skulked to the last line of shielding brush, Rosindo had known what to expect.

Dismounting with his Winchester, he had crept to the cliff's edge. As his father had taught him, he had knelt in the snow and planted the butt against his shoulder. Watching down the sights, he had waited for his chance to free his father's *bulto* from its restless wandering.

But Rosindo had failed, and all he could do now was lever another cartridge into the chamber and hope that *el oso plateado* would reemerge.

It didn't happen. The two riders below maintained vigilance for an hour before the older man swiped one hand across the other, apparently simulating the bear's flight, and pointed down-canyon. Soon the hunters rode on in that direction.

During the wait, Rosindo had repeatedly cautioned Benita to silence with gestures. For the most part, she had complied. But when the muchacho started back to where she stood beside the roan, Benita sobbed a truth that he couldn't deny.

"It's cold! The wind's cold!"

"I know, my sister."

"Do something, Rosindo! Make it stop!"

Already, she was wrapped in a colorful woolen serape, but as he came up before her and tucked it around her neck, her flushed face and frightful shiver alarmed him. For the moment, he couldn't worry about the bear. If he didn't act quickly, he might lose more than a chance to see their father in Heaven.

Boosting Benita into the saddle, he led the roan down the slope away from the cliff to a level spot on the lee of a pinyon with shrubby underbrush. Here, mountain mahogany and arroyo willow grew among the climbing vines of a wild grape and formed a windbreak. Upon tying the horse and helping his sister dismount, Rosindo set about gathering fuel. Finding dry wood and tinder wasn't easy, but down in the understory he found deadfall and grass protected from the elements.

"Hurry!" begged Bonita, who stood hunched. "Make it stop! Make the cold stop!"

The muchacho worked diligently, but even with fire-making tools from the saddle, everything was a challenge with numb fingers. With the strike of his skinning knife on flint, he tried again and again to ignite a small nest of grass before a spark landed just right. Even so, only by gently blowing did he keep the fledgling blaze alive long enough to slip it under a tepee of kindling and start a fire. For this knowledge, and so much more, Rosindo was thankful that he had learned at the feet of his *papá*.

As the fire crackled and threw out welcome heat, he had to restrain Benita from standing too close.

"But I'm cold, Rosindo!"

"You must give it time." He took one of her small hands and rubbed it between his. "Warm up, little *mano*! Warm up!"

"The other one!" she implored when he stopped. "Do the other one!"

Rosindo obliged, and when Benita warmed to the point that she no longer complained, he dragged up a dry log on which she could sit and then unsaddled the horse. In early morning, the roan had watered at a spring, but the boy regretted that the snow deprived the animal of forage. All he could do was rub the horse down with bunched grass and clean its feet. He had already lifted a forefoot and was about to scrape the hoof with a pick when his sister spoke.

"I saw him, Rosindo."

The muchacho turned. "What?"

"Up higher, waiting for you, I saw Papá."

Rosindo lowered the roan's leg and studied her as she stared into the fire.

"When I closed my eyes," continued Benita, "I could see him in black clothes. I couldn't see his face, but it was Papá."

Rosindo went nearer. He had hoped his sister would be spared looking upon their father's *bulto,* but the man in black had shown himself to her while denying Rosindo a glimpse for days now.

"Did he say anything, my sister?"

"He waved like he wanted me to follow him and went away."

"Show me."

Twisting around, the girl pointed in the direction that the two hunters had ridden. All the muchacho could see was blowing snow, thicker than ever, but he remembered from the day before that the range's highest peaks lay along the same course.

"Papá . . . Papá . . ." A sob entered the girl's voice. "Why did I see him?"

"He . . . He's not at rest," said Rosindo. "Remember what the *curandero* said? He's taking us to the great bear."

"Papá . . . I want Papá!"

So did Rosindo, more than anything, and abruptly all the matters he couldn't understand descended on his shoulders in a crushing burden. Sinking to the log through a blurry world, he drew his sobbing sister close and remembered the padre telling of a great king's words upon losing his son.

"Papá can never come back to us," whispered Rosindo. "But we can go to him."

And when he closed his eyes, Rosindo once again saw their father, a black form sharply contrasted against pristine snow as he beckoned the boy to follow.

CHAPTER NINE

It was the kind of cold that could peel the flesh from a person's face.

Until the wind had picked up, Grace had been uncomfortable, even chilled, but now the cold seemed to cut through her marrow. Shivering, she rode hunched over the saddle horn, her face down and the whipping collar of her jacket over her ears. With every breath, her sinuses burned, and the pain extended all the way to her raw throat. Worst of all was a numbness that left her feeling detached at times, as if she drifted in and out of her own body.

"Can't stand it! Can't stand it!"

From the dapple gray just ahead, Tommy ranted, his speech thick.

"I can't! I can't! I can't!"

Grace understood, for she was more than miserable. For the last few minutes, she had feared that she would die.

When neither Trey nor her father had come back up the gully, she and Tommy had taken their horses on along the narrow shelf. Now, they were bunched up against Isom and Mulholland, the four horses and the bull terriers moving single-file on a course more treacherous than ever, with an unscalable rise on the right and a sharp drop on the left. Snow blew so furiously that she seemed suspended in a white sea that denied more than fleeting hints of the way ahead.

"Can't stand it! Can't stand it!" continued Tommy.

The way he flailed and bounced in the saddle worried Grace. In these conditions, his horse had to be as skittish as hers, and with a single misstep on the icy shelf, the dapple gray could plunge with him into the unknown.

"You've got to calm down, Tommy!" Grace's deadened lips and tongue slurred her words.

"Can't stand it, Little Miss! Can't stand it!"

"Think about your horse—you're spooking him," she pleaded. "You don't want to cause him to hurt himself."

Where her plea for Tommy's self-control failed, her appeal for the welfare of his horse succeeded. Almost immediately, the man settled down in the saddle and patted the dapple gray on the neck.

"Easy, boy, you's all right, all right," he told the horse. "I give you your head and you be all right, for sure."

Leaning to the side to see past Tommy's shoulder, Grace could barely discern Mulholland's outline on the animal ahead of Isom.

"We've got to get off this mountain!" she shouted. "Mr. Mulholland, you've got to find a way down!"

But the hazy figure gave no indication that he had heard over the rush of the wind, and she tried another tack.

"Tommy, tell him what I said."

"Mean man won't listen. Mr. Wash tell him, 'Don't beat that dog,' and he go on and do it anyhow. Awful mean man!"

"This is different, Tommy. He's got to be looking for a way to get us out of the wind. He's not doing your horse fair, none of the horses fair."

Once more, her petition for the well-being of a horse worked. Again, Tommy patted the dapple gray.

"Poor things just a-sufferin', this ol' wind. Wasn't for us, they'd be somewheres they could turn away and bury their ol' heads between their knees."

"Then tell him," urged Grace. "Tell Mr. Mulholland the horses can't take any more of this. Tell him I said to look for a way off this mountain."

For a few seconds, she heard Tommy merely grumble, something about the mean man who had beaten Sleuth. But just as she was about to implore Tommy again, he called through the storm.

"Little Trey's pappy! Little Trey's pappy! Little Miss say tell you, 'Watch for a way down! Horses a-sufferin'! Watch for a way down!' "

Mulholland's indistinct figure twisted about, followed by words Grace couldn't distinguish.

"What did he say?" she asked Tommy.

"I told you he a mean man!" Tommy replied. " 'Quit your damned jabberin'!' he says. 'What in hell you *think* I'm doin'?' Awful mean man!"

All Grace could do was bow her head, scrunch her shoulders against the cold, and let the roan carry her where it would. For minutes or hours she rode with eyes closed, swaying with the horse's gentle gait. She grew strangely oblivious to the elements, and as she drifted away with increasing frequency, a baffling contentment came over her. Numb to everything, she wanted to sleep the long sleep, to accept the peaceful rest, but from a corner of her mind her six-year-old self told her that she mustn't yet.

Kill him. For Papa, you've got to kill him.

She listened, even though it would have been so much easier to drift and drift and drift . . .

Distantly, she realized the horse had stopped, and she opened her eyes to the other riders and the bull terriers framed inside an icy glade, a small flat bounded by dense pinyons. Here, somewhere off the exposed slope, the wind had relented, and only a few swirling flakes added to a blanket of snow that rose halfway to the horses' knees. Already, the pine limbs sagged under their white loads, and the pliable stalks of frosted ocotillo drooped even more.

Just past a stand of agave with snow cradled between its spiny pads, Mulholland was trying to dismount, but his legs evidently wouldn't cooperate.

"Give me a hand here! I'm froze to my horse!"

Had he been anyone but Mulholland, Grace would have commiserated. Only by checking down along her own unresponsive leg could she confirm that her step-off foot was still in the stirrup.

"I ain't helpin' mean man!" said Tommy, struggling off his dapple gray.

"Damn it!" added Mulholland, "I got to get off of this horse!"

As he railed on, Grace pressed down on her saddle horn and cantle and relieved the pressure against one leg and then the other. Circulation began to return, but even after swinging off into the snow, she kept a steadying hand on the roan.

Meanwhile, Isom had dismounted and now he assisted Mulholland, who continued to swear from the saddle. Grace might have left him there, but in these conditions, all of them needed to band together.

"Can't stand it! Can't stand it!" complained Tommy, massaging the back of his thigh as he stood with his horse. He looked around at Mulholland. "Listen to that mean man cuss, Little Miss!"

Grace couldn't worry about a breach in propriety, or the fact that Mulholland doubtless had heard Tommy's epithet for him. They were all half-frozen and had to act quickly, decisively, but there seemed no one to take charge.

"We've got to build a fire!" she shouted. "Brother Isom, you and Mr. Mulholland find wood! Tommy, take care of the horses!"

Grace was just a girl, but the three men responded, even Mulholland once he was down and his legs worked again. Not a moment too soon, Grace and Isom dug into a big rat's nest under the thick limbs of a left-side pinyon and found not only dry tinder, but deadfall large enough to sustain a fire. As everyone gathered, Mulholland awkwardly extended a match to the clergyman.

"Damned hand's like a ham hock," said Mulholland. "Squat down and get a fire goin'."

But Isom's fingers must have had just as little feeling. Unable to grasp the match normally, he closed the bottom of his fist around it and struck the exposed head on a log. When it failed to ignite, he tried a second time, a third, and repeated the futile process when Mulholland produced additional matches.

"Damned things is wet!" exclaimed Mulholland. "Who else has got any?"

Maybe Grace had been too reliant on others in the hunt, for she had failed to bring matches of her own. But as Isom displayed his empty hands to Mulholland, and Tommy began to panic, she remembered something she had learned from her father.

"Don't waste any more!" she warned Mulholland. "May I have one?"

With a match in hand, she twirled it in her hair, close to the scalp. She persisted even as Mulholland scoffed and he demanded that Isom strike again and again, until the match heads surely disintegrated. When the clergyman exhausted the supply, Grace could see fear in all of their eyes. With Mulholland swearing indiscriminately, she protected the dried match with a cupped hand and knelt to the tinder.

"Brother Isom," she said, "this would be a good time for a prayer."

But Isom's remarks weren't what she expected.

"Judgment, righteous judgment," said the preacher. " 'He casteth forth his ice like morsels: who can stand before his cold?' "

With her own silent prayer, Grace struck the match. It flared immediately, but she endured anxious moments before the tinder began to smolder. Nothing burned easily in the mountains, and she had to nurture the fledgling fire with gentle breaths until wispy flames lapped the wood.

As everyone crowded around and Mulholland stoked the blaze, Grace thought about Trey and her father. Never had a fire felt so good, and the difference between the warmth at her breast and the cold at her back was dramatic. Just a few feet away, conditions were so brutal that even the bull terriers had been drawn to the fire. A person could die out there; indeed, she had *expected* to meet her end on that mountainside, and she trembled when she considered the fate of the two men for whom she cared most.

Cared most.

Grace looked across the fire at Trey's father, struck by how he seemed to stand in the very flames. The rising smoke swept around his shoulders and enveloped him as if he already burned in hell for his role in Joe's death. For Trey's sake, Grace feared the power of the whispering voice from her childhood.

She continued to study Mulholland as he reached inside his coat and withdrew something on a leather boot lace looped around his neck. Pivoting from the campfire, he blew a police whistle, the two-note blast shrill even in the heavy air. Continuing to revolve in place, he repeated the process until the summons had gone out across the four points of the compass.

"Where the hell's them dogs of mine?" he brooded out loud.

"Poor ol' Sleuth," lamented Tommy, casting his eyes back across the meadow. "He mine, I sure treat him right."

"Yeah, well, he *ain't* yours," snapped Mulholland.

Once more, he blew his whistle in every direction and then cupped a hand alongside his mouth.

"Come here, you mangy devils!" he shouted, his breath a vapor in the cold.

"Poor ol' Sleuth," repeated Tommy. "He sure a good dog to have a mean man ownin' him."

For anyone who knew better, it was an intemperate remark, and as Mulholland faced the fire, he gave Tommy a brief look that Grace didn't like. For a while, the older man seemed content to rub his hands together and hold them out to catch the warmth. Then with a loud belch, he gained everyone's attention.

"All of you better watch it, a freeze like this," he said as if holding court before his subjects. "I was out there in eighty-four, what they call the big drift when them cattle come out of the north. Awfullest blizzard I ever seen. If you let your toes go numb, they's liable to get hard like a block of ice. You can even walk a little, but when they go to thawin' out, you ain't never felt the pain. Come spring, summer, you'll lose them toes, sure as hell."

He paused and looked again at Tommy before reiterating his unsolicited advice.

"Yeah, all of you better watch it."

If his intent was to alarm Tommy in retribution, he succeeded.

"L-Little Miss?" Tommy stood at Grace's immediate left. "I ain't felt my toes all day. I . . . I goin' to lose them?"

"Don't worry, Tommy," she said. "We've got a warm fire now."

"But he say—"

"I know what he said. Just stay by the fire. You'll be all right."

Mulholland snorted. "The hell he will if he don't watch it. Won't be like a grizzly growin' its four-inch claws back neither.

He'll be hobblin' around on a couple of stumps if them toes rot off."

Tommy began to flail his arms and stalk around away from the fire. "He say it! Mean man say it! He say I goin' to lose them!"

Tommy always wore his boots outside his pants legs, and if anything would increase the likelihood of frostbite, it was ice packing his uppers every time he stamped his feet down in a deep drift.

Mulholland's doing, every bit of it.

They had been her father's words about the tragedy, and they were Grace's words now, although under her breath.

She stepped away from the fire, feeling the bite of the cold, and took Tommy by the arm.

"Come stand by me, Tommy."

"Mean man say—"

Grace tugged. "Come on over where it's warm and tell me about that blazed-face chestnut you broke for Papa."

Her ploy worked.

"He sure goin' to be a good one, Little Miss," he said as he accompanied her back to the fire.

Once there, Grace checked his boots. As she feared, the uppers were crusted with snow.

"Tommy, let's get the ice out of your boots. Pull off one at a time. Here, hold to my shoulder."

As she assisted, Grace talked with him about the young horse. Soon his boots were back on.

"Your feet feel better already, don't they?" asked Grace, wanting to plant the idea in his mind.

"They do, Little Miss. They—"

"Yeah, come spring, we'll see," interrupted Mulholland. "Be like the Montana cowboy makin' fun of the way Texas boys tie their catch-ropes hard and fast. He cut two fingers off, dallyin'

101

his rope around the saddle horn. It was 'dally, then tally.' Except in your case, it won't be tallyin' up the fingers you got left. It'll be tallyin' the toes you lost."

Tommy started flailing his arms again, and only Grace's grip on his shoulder kept him from pacing once more in the snow.

Grace glared at Mulholland. "Is that how you did it?"

"Did what?"

Got my brother killed! Destroyed Papa to where he has to live with the guilt every day! Ruined any chance with him for Trey and me!

Grace wanted to say these things and more, but her six-year-old self told her there would be a time for that later.

"If a person let you," she said instead, "you'd have them in such a panic, somebody would be sure to get hurt."

"Just tellin' what I know," said Mulholland.

Grace could see her father's face buried in his hands as he wept on the mountainside.

"I . . . I guess you know everything, don't you." *About bears! About man-killers! About what to do if something comes at you in the dark!*

"Pays to listen," said Mulholland.

For a moment, Grace was a small girl again, squeezing the trigger of a six-shooter as she whispered *Mulholland! Mulholland!*

"I listened," said Isom, who had not spoken since quoting Scripture to Grace. "I listened to the child crying. He was crying and crying and crying, until he didn't cry anymore."

"How come poor thing takin' on so?" asked Tommy.

"You remember, Tommy," interjected Grace. "He took sick and died."

"Lost his mama first, poor thing," acknowledged Tommy. "Like the Appaloosy leavin' the dogie foal. I was up all night tendin' the little thing, but didn't do no good."

" 'To die is gain,' " quoted Isom.

When Grace studied the clergyman across the snapping fire, he had the same lost look that she had seen in her father's face—and in Trey's ever since they had gathered for the hunt.

Mulholland's police whistle wouldn't let her reflect for long. Maybe it was the elevation, or perhaps the cold made everything worse, but even as Grace turned away, her ears began to ring—even ache—to the piercing summons.

This time, however, hounds answered from the distance. Over the next ten minutes, with a "call and response" method like Isom's sermons before tragedy had subdued his zeal, Mulholland guided the dogs closer until the reddish-brown female and the two black-and-tan males broke through the pinyons across the glade.

"Where's good ol' dog Sleuth?" pondered Tommy.

"Hell, no tellin'," said Mulholland.

With the bull terriers at his heels, Mulholland met the hounds at his horse. After taking up his quirt, evidently to keep the terriers from fighting, he began tossing out strips of jerky from the saddlebag, only to turn at Tommy's exclamation.

"Here comes poor ol' dog!"

Surely enough, appearing from a totally different direction than the other hounds, Sleuth came bounding through the snow with something furry between his slobbering jaws.

"You worthless outfit!" said Mullholland. "Send you after a bear and you go runnin' a damned jackrabbit. Get yourself over here!"

Chastised, Sleuth stopped and lowered his head. Only after another summons did he slowly slink forward, the loose folds of his tawny red coat quivering and the floppy ears dragging the snow. Mulholland met him halfway and tried to yank the kill out of his jaws.

"Drop the damned thing!"

When Sleuth relaxed his hold, Mulholland tossed the rabbit

aside and the snarling terriers converged on it, smearing the snow with the rabbit's blood as they contended. Meanwhile, Sleuth, as docile as ever, cowered submissively before Mulholland.

"I told you I'd teach you!" said Mulholland.

With one hand he grabbed Sleuth by the big brass buckle on the three-inch-wide leather collar, and with the other he quirted the dog unmercifully.

"Mean man! Mean man!" cried Tommy, going wild again.

It was pitiful, hearing the dog yelp as the rawhide braids fell, the cracks sharp in the cold air. Grace started for Mulholland, but the words on her lips were drowned out by a shout from behind.

"No more! Not another lick more!"

Whirling, Grace saw an Appaloosa with her father astride emerge from the pinyons, followed by Trey on his dun.

"What the hell?" exclaimed Mulholland.

Her father brought his horse closer. "Makes three times I've watched you whip that dog. I'm not putting up with it anymore."

In the cold, his diction was poor, but Mulholland understood plainly enough.

"*My* dog, Baker. Shut up and mind your own damned business."

"I'll make it my business if you hit that dog again. That's not trainin' or discipline. It's downright cruelty, and I'm not standin' for it, here on out."

Mulholland tightened his grip on the collar. "Then we got us a real row comin'. I'll treat him any damned way I want. Long as he's mine, you ain't got a say in hell."

Grace's father pulled rein directly above the man. "All right, what do you want for him?"

"What the hell you sayin'?"

"I'll buy him off of you. How much he worth?"

"Damned thing ain't worth nothin' to me." Mulholland shoved the dog toward the Appaloosa, spooking the horse a little. "You want him that bad, you take him then. Just don't come cryin' to me if you ain't got nothin' to feed him."

Withdrawing, Mulholland swore viciously at the other dogs and tossed more jerky on the snow.

Grace, who had stopped halfway to the scene, heard the squeak and jangle of a saddle behind her.

"I'm sorry, Miss Grace. He doesn't have any right to speak that way in front of you."

Checking, she found the dun with Trey in the stirrups. A blood-soaked bandana lay in a band across his forehead, and more blood had dried in a stream down his frosted cheek.

"Trey! What's happened?"

But now that he'd had his say, the young man reined the dun aside and urged it toward the other horses. Reminded of all she may have lost, Grace turned with the dun's course and saw that her father had stepped off his Appaloosa and was down in the snow with the hound. Sleuth, meek but not fearful, nuzzled his fingers.

"I told you you'd made a friend, Papa," she said as she approached.

Her father glanced up. "He needs one, if a dog ever did."

He ran his hand gently along the hound's baggy hide, the short coat showing the ugly marks of every lash—even one across the eye.

"I know you's hurtin'," he told Sleuth. "Joe would've . . ." He found a deep breath, and for a moment, Grace didn't think he could continue. "He . . . He would've sure took on about you."

Grace had never heard her father speak of Joe so openly, and he suddenly seemed a lost, lonely figure standing like a scarecrow in a past filled with regret. The snowpack rose above his boot tops, and the drifting flakes dusted a face already crusted with frost, and yet he seemed not to realize that a winter storm had him in its grip while a campfire crackled from so near.

She took his arm. "Papa, you're freezing. Come on over by the fire."

Her tug shook him into awareness, for he smoothed his hand over the dog's head. "I can barely take care of myself out in all this. Don't know how I'll look after him too."

Grace glanced at the fire. "Tommy's dying to." Then she called. "Tommy, come here a minute!"

From several yards out in the snow, Tommy was already looking on expectantly, and he came rushing across.

"Mean man whipped him somethin' awful, poor ol' thing!"

"Won't happen anymore," Wash told Tommy as he arrived. "Sleuth's mine."

"Yours, Mr. Wash? He yours now?"

"Remember that yellow hound that Joe . . ." Emotion overcame Wash. "He always looked after the old thing. I . . . I need . . ."

When his voice choked, Grace spoke up. "He wants you to take care of Sleuth, Tommy. Think you can do that?"

Grace had never seen his face light up so. His eyebrows lifted, his eyes went round, and a huge grin parted his lips. Dropping down in the snow, he started to hug the dog.

"Don't squeeze too hard, Tommy," warned her father, finding his voice. "He's pretty tender."

"Good ol' dog!" said Tommy, his spittle flying in his excitement. He patted the hound gently. "You's just like me. Got you a good home with Mr. Wash 'stead of that mean man!"

"Tommy," said Grace, "take Papa's reins and look after his horse. He needs to get over to the fire."

Her father's legs were so stiff that she had to help him as they started across the snow.

"Papa, what happened to Trey, blood on his face that way?"

"Near got killed. Found him danglin' off a cliff, just his reins holdin' him."

"Papa!" she gasped.

Suddenly Grace couldn't breathe. Her heart began to pound, and she needed a supporting arm more than he did.

"Knew you'd be upset," he said. "Rather not have said nothin', but his face tells it all."

Upon reaching the fire, Wash nodded in greeting to Isom and propped up a foot on a log just outside the flames.

"Barely feel my toes anymore," he remarked.

With his boot out of the snow, Grace saw deep slash marks across the upper.

"Your boot's all cut up!" she said. "What kind of brush did you and Trey ride through?"

With a furtive glance at her, he lowered his foot and concealed the upper in the snow again.

"Papa?"

His chest rose. "Figured all of you done knew."

"What do you mean?"

Now he turned. "How'd you and Tommy wind up with Brother Isom and Mulholland? Been wonderin' how somebody got across that deep canyon."

"Nobody crossed it, Papa. We caught up with them on the mountain and ended up here."

Her father frowned and addressed Isom across the fire. "Y'all didn't do any shootin'?"

"What I hunt for doesn't require a gun, Brother Baker."

Wash looked down and tugged on his earlobe. "*Somebody* sure fired a shot, right down where we was at in the canyon. Trey swore it come from up across."

"Someone else was out in this?" Grace asked in surprise. Then she grew concerned. "What were they shooting at?"

For the second time, her father didn't answer, choosing instead to stir the fire with a stick. Except where Joe was concerned, it wasn't like him to be so uncommunicative.

"Papa . . ." Grace glanced at his hidden boot and remembered Mulholland's description. "Did it have something to do with the way your boot's sliced up?"

Clearly, he was reluctant to answer. He poked the fire again, causing sparks to rise.

"Glad y'all got a fire goin'," he said. "Never seen the like of weather to be November."

Grace pressed the issue. "Mr. Mulholland said a grizzly's got claws four inches long."

"Yeah, Mulholland's not shy about talkin'."

It was neither confirmation nor a denial, and Grace knew him well enough not to ask again. For a while she stood at the fire as the flames crawled across wood that sizzled and popped. Repeatedly she glanced at Trey, who lingered in front of his dun despite the frigid conditions. Then Tommy came up alongside her with Sleuth, and when Mulholland joined Isom across the fire, Grace started across the snow for the horses.

As she neared, Trey's lips were moving silently as he stroked the dun's face. He must have heard her, for he glanced around and then shifted so that his features were hidden.

The hurt mounted.

"Aren't . . . Aren't you coming to the fire?" Grace asked quietly.

He muttered something she couldn't distinguish.

"It . . . It's cold out here," she added. "Why don't you come get warm?"

She stepped around so that she could look at him, but as he had done the night before, he turned away more so that she could see only his shoulders—shoulders that blurred as her eyes welled.

"Trey . . ." What Grace would have given to have things back the way they had been. "Papa says you almost got killed."

"Killed," he whispered. "Like Joe."

After going her entire life with hearing scarcely a mention of her brother's death, the tragedy strangely seemed to be on the minds of so many. Her eyes stinging, Grace put her hand on Trey's arm, only to have him subtly draw away. Crushed, she supposed it was over between them, but there was something else that also concerned her.

"Tell me what happened to Papa's boot."

As if in surprise, Trey started to glance back and then hesitated. "You don't know?" he asked quietly.

"No, and Papa won't say."

"Then it was one of the others. Father maybe. Ask him."

Grace grew even more confused. "Ask him what? Papa did say there was a gunshot, but none of us been shooting."

Again, Trey's head turned a little. "Peculiar. Shot's the only thing that spared him."

"Spared him what, Trey? Please tell me."

"If you saw his boot . . ." He bowed his head. "By rights, should have been me. Both times, me. Instead . . ."

He whispered a word that could have been *Joe,* and then his shoulders began to shake.

CHAPTER TEN

Stark against pure white, the blood spots laid a trail even more striking than the tracks set deeply in the snow.

With a stride twice that of a man, *el oso plateado* had come this way, each hind foot overstepping the one in front. Had Rosindo walked instead of ridden, the rear imprints would have swallowed his huaraches, and the extended claw marks rendered the front tracks almost as long. The natural spoor was intimidating, but the drip line of blood worried the muchacho more, for he remembered his father warning of the danger of an animal merely wounded by a bullet.

For minutes, Rosindo and Benita had warmed by the fire and partaken of nourishment. Then the blizzard had broken, and the spirit figure in black and the approach of the full moon beyond the snow clouds had lured Rosindo on. With Benita snuggled against his back and each of them wrapped in multiple layers of serapes, the muchacho had taken the roan through stands of snow-powdered ponderosas and across fields of glazed boulders, and along an icy ridge and down a pinyon-studded grade into a tangled drainage. There, the hoofs had broken though a frozen pool that had allowed animal and riders alike to drink between the floating leafage of autumn—the crimson leaves of gray oaks and the yellow foliage of black cherries.

Now they navigated a narrow gulch defined on the right by alligator junipers with a thick understory of buckeye, hackberry, and mountain mahogany, and bordered on the left by a steep rise.

Benita began to sob.

"What's wrong?" asked Rosindo.

He felt her head press against his shoulder and her arms tighten around him.

"Benita?"

She squeezed even more, enabling him to feel her fitful gasps as she wept.

"Are you cold again?" he asked. "What is it?"

"I . . . I'm scared, Rosindo," she managed.

"What are you afraid of?"

"I don't want you to die!"

Rosindo pulled rein and turned in the saddle as best he could with Benita still clinging.

"I'm right here, my sister. I'm not going anywhere."

"You don't know that, Rosindo! You don't know! Papá didn't know, and he died and left us!"

The muchacho's eyes began to smart.

"I won't have anybody!" Benita continued. "You'll die like Papá and I won't have anybody!"

Rosindo didn't know what to tell her, and as she grew silent, grieving in her tiny heart for what the future might hold, he rode on through a world that now seemed lonelier than ever without their father.

For long minutes, the way seemed darker and darker before the muchacho suddenly grew alarmed, something beyond his senses alerting him to be on guard. To the groan of saddle leather, he checked left and right, ahead and behind. He found nothing unexpected, but the feeling was still there, growing stronger with every pace of the roan.

He reached for the rusty carbine under his leg and, with fingers stiffened by cold, began fumbling with the saddle strings that held it in place. He didn't want to make a show, not only for Benita's sake, but for whatever eyes seemed to be watching.

His gaze was drawn to the wall of brush on the right, and he reined up and heard a brief stirring of leaves and then silence. He took the roan a few paces farther and stopped again, this time hearing the faint crack of a limb. For a third time, he squeezed the horse with his thighs and proceeded on, only to hear a momentary rustle when he drew rein.

Something was there.

Flanking them inside the timber.

Moving when they moved, and stopping when they stopped.

Even as Rosindo redoubled his efforts to free the carbine, he fought to control his emotions, not wanting to exhibit concern either to Benita or to whatever stalked them. He remembered what his father had taught him: An animal could sense fear, and when it did, it triggered a predatory response that could overcome its instinctive dread of man and embolden an attack.

But this was the moment of truth. His mind might tell him what he should do, but his body didn't seem his to control. He could hear his own short, rapid breaths and the rhythmic thud in his chest, and as a shudder seized him he could no longer worry about how he might be perceived.

The great bear had circled back and was poised to charge.

"Rosindo . . . Rosindo . . . ?"

Even if Benita didn't feel him shaking, his frantic efforts to free the carbine were enough to alarm her. When the knots remained stubborn and he saw movement through the under-story, the muchacho did the only thing he could—he gigged the horse with a cry.

"Vamos!"

The horse jumped forward through deep snow that flew from its hoofs. For stride after stride through impeding drifts, the horse lunged with leaden forefeet, a pace so slow that Rosindo

112

could almost feel the bear's claws dragging him down from behind.

"Rosindo! Rosindo!"

"Hold to me!" he yelled.

But Rosindo himself rocked violently to the roan's leaping gait, and when the boy's foot slipped free, he fell forward across the animal's neck and listed toward the flopping stirrup.

"Rosindo!"

For a moment the muchacho was more off than on, but somehow he clutched the streaming mane and righted himself. It had been a close call worthy of Benita's cry of sheer terror, but maybe they would make it.

And then he realized that his sister's arms were no longer around him, and that only the cantle of the saddle was at his back.

"Benita!"

Rosindo wheeled the horse and saw his sister sprawled, her dark hair disheveled against the snow. In moments he was back up trail and down beside her, calling her name and glancing through the roan's legs at the understory that hid too much.

The bear was there! A hazy outline through the limbs! It would explode out of hackberry and buckeye and they would have no more chance than their *papá*!

"Benita! Benita!"

She stirred and he put his arms under her shoulders.

"Quick!" he cried. *"Vaya con prisa!"*

But she was shaken and didn't seem to understand, and all he could do was try to drag her up while maintaining a tenuous hold on the reins.

A woman screamed, rocking the gulch.

The woman screamed again, and Benita came alive.

"Rosindo! Rosindo!"

At the same instant, the horse bolted, jerking the reins from the muchacho's hold, and he was left to whirl to the brush and find the one who had shrieked.

It wasn't a woman. It wasn't *el oso plateado.* Through a break in the timber, he saw a long, tawny figure, three feet high at the muscled shoulder, switching its dark-tipped tail and panting.

Madre de Dios, a mountain lion!

The cat took a slinking step toward them, and then another and another, parting the limbs of buckeye and mountain mahogany until they faced each other from yards apart. Rosindo had helped trap and skin lions for years, and this was as large as any he had seen, its greenish-gold eyes dominating the round head. With ears laid back in readiness to pounce, the cat stared with evil intent, and the muchacho remembered what his father had said.

A mountain lion might track a man out of curiosity, but attacks were rare. *If ever confronted, make yourself big.*

Desperate, Rosindo quickly picked up his panicked sister. Perching her on his hip, he yelled over her terrified cries.

"Raise your arms! Raise your arms!"

He must have said it a dozen times, even after Benita had complied, and between their shouts and the intimidating size the two of them presented, the lion spooked and ran away.

"I want to go home! I want to go home!"

It was all that Benita seemed able to say as Rosindo lowered her to the snow and took stock of their situation. Now that the danger had passed, he was so weak that he quaked. He didn't think he could ever be this scared again, but as he turned with a changing breeze and sighted the strayed horse, he found a reason.

From somewhere near came a roar that had to be *el oso plateado.*

"Storm's done blowed through. See them clouds? Ain't even

the kind it snows from."

Now that everyone had gathered at the fire, Wash stood listening to Mulholland lecture on the latest topic on which he was an authority. Wash didn't bother looking across at him, choosing instead to peer into the glowing coals. But when Mulholland hiked his leg and passed gas—and called attention to it by grunting "there's more room on the outside than on the inside"—Wash lifted his eyes. Grace remained expressionless, but Trey obviously was dismayed, for his lower lip pushed up and he shook his head.

"Baker," said the elder Mulholland, "you and my boy gallivantin' off like you done, come across any bear sign?"

When Wash didn't answer, Mulholland turned to Trey. "You need to stick with me and you might learn somethin' about huntin' grizzlies. Why, off up yonder in Colorado—"

Trey said something, but the way his father rambled on, no one could possibly have understood. When Mulholland paused for a breath, Trey spoke up again.

"Father," he said impatiently, "it pays to know when to be quiet and listen."

Mulholland drew back, clearly surprised and more than a little perturbed. "Hell, take the reins if you got somethin' worth sayin'."

"After somebody shot down in the canyon where we were, we—"

"Shot?" interrupted Mulholland in surprise. "Wasn't nobody from *our* bunch. Who the hell shot?"

Undeterred, Trey continued, "—we spent a long time catching Mr. Baker's horse. But when we rode on, we heard a roar off to the north like we heard on Sawtooth yesterday."

"North, huh?" said Mulholland.

"We'd seen the smoke from the fire and knew we needed to warm up and rest the horses. But it's not more than a mile back to where we heard it."

"Hell," said his father, "take me over there and I'll turn my dogs loose. We got some daylight left. I'm losin' money ever' time that bear gets hungry."

CHAPTER ELEVEN

Below Wash's stirrup and seated boot, Sleuth whined as he watched the other bloodhounds zigzag across the snow with their noses down in search of a hot trail.

Moments ago in this small clearing, Mulholland had shouted "Go on!," and the reddish-brown female and a black-and-tan male had started away to the north, sweeping the drifts with their floppy ears. The third hound, with a white-tipped tail, had required coaxing—if swear words and a brandished quirt could be called coaxing—but now all three dogs were disappearing into pinyons heavy with snow.

The muscles under Sleuth's baggy hide quivered. He whined again, and when Wash reached down from the saddle, the hound nuzzled his fingers and then turned away with another note of sadness.

"Poor ol' dog," Tommy sympathized from his dapple gray. "He can't stand watchin', the poor ol' dog."

When Sleuth slobbered against Wash's hand again, Wash motioned toward the pinyons.

"Go on, far as you want to," he told the dog. "Won't be anybody whippin' you when you get back."

Sleuth understood, for he came to life. With muzzle down and tail curved over his back, he struck out eagerly along the tracks laid by the other hounds. Wash figured that even a blind man, if he stayed close enough, could follow the long, swinging streamers that Sleuth left in his wake.

"He sure a happy thing now, Mr. Wash!" exclaimed Tommy. "Look at ol' dog go!"

But Wash's focus was drawn to Tommy, who leaned forward over his dapple gray's neck to watch Sleuth from a little closer. Wash didn't think he had ever seen Tommy so elated, for his green eyes crinkled and a wide grin flashed his stained teeth.

"Fed him out of your own jerky, didn't you, Tommy?"

Tommy continued to stare after the hound, who now had a more pronounced catch in his stride. "Ol' Sleuth, he need it more than me. Look at him go!"

There was something about Tommy's connection with Sleuth that touched Wash inside. The two of them, dog and man, had much in common. One was a gentle, loveable animal who had been mistreated and spurned, and the other a tenderhearted soul who had known only rejection and abuse as a child. Wash had rescued both of them, in a way, but he abruptly wished that he had done more for Tommy, who would always face challenges in life. He couldn't imagine where a person with his handicap would end up once he and Emma were gone.

"Tommy," he said, "you love that old dog, don't you."

"He a good one, ol' Sleuth is."

"You love that blazed-face chestnut you broke for me, too."

The mention of the young horse may have been the only thing that could redirect Tommy's attention.

"He be the best cow pony ever, sure 'nough," he said, making eye contact.

"You been with me a lot of years, Tommy. Tell you what I'm goin' to do. I'm givin' you that horse, free and clear."

If Tommy had seemed happy before, it was nothing compared to the excitement and joy he showed now. His eyebrows shot up and stayed there, rounded arches over eyes that seemed almost as large as the dapple gray's.

"You mean it, Mr. Wash? You mean it? You mean it? You really mean it?"

"I sure do, Tommy. He's yours, now on."

Tommy spun to Grace on her roan. "You hear, Little Miss? You hear what Mr. Wash done for me?"

"I *heard*, Tommy," she replied, celebrating with him. "A horse of your very own!"

As Grace looked at Wash, the delight in her face almost equaled Tommy's, and Wash realized that he didn't have to worry anymore about Tommy's welfare once the gravediggers called. But Tommy, true to his ways, didn't know when to leave well enough alone.

"Just think, Little Miss!" he mused. "I got me my own cow pony and get to look after poor ol' dog that no mean man ever goin' to whip again!"

Mulholland had already urged his sorrel after the hounds, but Wash saw him glance back with a scowl that no one like Tommy deserved.

Falling in behind, Wash found Isom riding abreast on his left, the two of them apart from the others. The clergyman's black cutaway coat was striking against the snowy pinyons.

"Still awful cold, isn't it, Brother Isom," said Wash. "Sure felt good back at the fire."

Isom strangely rode with eyes closed. "Fire," he repeated in a low tone. " 'Where their worm dieth not, and the fire is not quenched.' "

"Thinkin' on your next sermon?"

"Fire." Isom continued to whisper as if to himself. "Where 'there shall be wailing and gnashing of teeth.' "

When he opened his eyes, his steel-wire spectacles seemed directed ahead at Mulholland as the older man and his sorrel weaved through the pinyons.

"How great must the sin be," asked Isom, as quietly as ever, "for Almighty God to cast a man into hell?"

"You's the preacher man," Wash answered. "Whatever it takes, I'd say Ed Mulholland's got a leg up."

Isom turned to him, confusion in his drawn features. "What?"

It was as though Isom hadn't heard anything Wash had said, and when the clergyman straightened in the saddle and again closed his eyes, Wash fixed his attention on Mulholland and rode on in silence.

After several minutes, a bark came from ahead, followed by one bark after another, and when Wash heard Sleuth's croak as well, he knew that the hounds had struck a hot trail. The chase was on, through slapping pinyon limbs that sprayed Wash's face with snow, through deep drifts in which his Appaloosa slogged, and across hidden deadfall that cracked and gave under the hoofs. He rode up and over one rise and then another, and through a wooded pass that opened to a gentle slope down through more pinyons with scattered redberry junipers and the autumn-bared skeletons of cottonwoods.

By the time the hounds began to bay in place, indicating that they had cornered their quarry, Wash had outdistanced Isom. Near a drainage, Wash bore left with the tracks along a bank with ash and bigtooth maple and a tangled understory of hackberry and mountain mahogany. A hundred yards farther, he drew rein under a huge gray oak beside a mounted Mulholland, who had his hat off as he dabbed his eye with his coat sleeve. Sleuth and the other hounds were looking up and baying constantly, while the growling terriers jumped at the tree in vain attempts to climb it.

Many of the scarlet leaves had fallen, and still others drifted down to the dogs. But forty or feet fifty up, the crown was dense, and Wash knew that something was there.

"Thought you said grizzlies don't tree," he said, peering up.

When Mulholland didn't answer, Wash turned and found him still tending his eye.

"What's the matter with you?" Wash asked.

"Caught a damned limb in my face." Mulholland looked up through the branches. "See him?"

"The grizzly?"

"Hell, told you they don't climb. You didn't see the tracks?"

"Not after you and the dogs tromped them out. What is it? Black bear?"

"A black bear seats himself on the first limb out of reach of the dogs. Only one thing climbs to the top. That's a lion up there."

Wash checked again, but even as he took the Appaloosa in a semicircle along the gray oak's drip line, he couldn't distinguish more than a dim outline behind all the leaves.

"Lost too many calves to them lions," said Mulholland. He slid his Krag .30-40 bolt-action rifle out of its saddle scabbard. "Here. Shoot him down out of there."

Wash reined his horse about and met him halfway. "How come you want me to do it? Shoot him yourself."

"Damned eye is waterin'. Come on, take this thing. You shoot him with that scattergun, liable to just make him mad."

Wash accepted the .30-40 and confirmed that a cartridge was in the chamber. He urged the Appaloosa forward and then circled back, searching the gray oak's crown all the while.

"Don't like shootin' somethin' I can't see," he said. Indeed, he had done so once before, and too many lives had changed because of it.

"Shoot the damned thing, Baker!"

Clicking off the safety, Wash seated the butt plate against his shoulder and captured the hazy form in the crimson foliage down the sights. When he squeezed the trigger, he rocked to the recoil and the Appaloosa shied, and the blast still rolled when something large dropped through the limbs and almost struck Sleuth and the hound with the white-tipped tail.

121

"Go ahead and wool the thing!" Mulholland shouted to his dogs.

But Sleuth must have learned something from experience in Tennessee, for as White Tip rushed in ahead of the terriers to maul the dead cat, the old hound withdrew.

Suddenly the lion came alive.

Lunging from where it sprawled, the cat seized White Tip by the throat with its jaws and dragged the dog down. The lion was up quickly, maintaining its asphyxiating grip as it struck lightning-fast with its paw at the snarling terriers as they arrived. The raking claws found their mark, but the terriers were as game as ever, pressing the attack from two sides.

"Kill it, Baker! Kill it!" yelled Mulholland.

But there was such a melee that Wash wouldn't shoot for fear of hitting a dog. Not only that, but the Appaloosa spooked and spun away, and when Wash reined the horse about, he saw the lion break free and run with the terriers in chase.

"Shoot it!" cried Mulholland.

But the lion didn't make it twenty yards before it collapsed, and just before the terriers overtook it and began to maul, Wash saw all the blood behind the cat's tawny shoulder. Wash's blind shot up into the gray oak had been deadly, but it had taken time.

White Tip was gravely wounded. Not only did the dog bleed profusely from the throat, but the lion must have crushed something inside, for it had a hard time breathing. Mulholland would have left White Tip where it lay or put a bullet through its head, but Wash couldn't forget Joe's attachment to the mangy yellow hound.

"Might get better if he's watched after," said Wash.

Mulholland protested, but Wash laid the dog across the front of his saddle and, with Sleuth hobbling behind, rode back the way they had come. With day fading fast, Wash had begun to shiver, and he knew that they better prepare for nightfall and the bitter cold it might bring. Mulholland had agreed that the glade where they had warmed by the blaze was a logical place, for it offered a windbreak and coals that might still ignite the abundant firewood.

Just as Wash came upon Isom, White Tip convulsed and died. Wash figured it was just as well; he couldn't imagine Tommy's pain if he had watched the animal suffer. Mulholland rode on by with his dogs, but with Isom's help, Wash buried the hound under deadfall as best he could.

Grace and the others must have turned back upon meeting Mulholland, for when Wash and Isom rode in with Sleuth, everyone was gathered around the smoking fire. Tommy's face lighted up as he came running out to the hound.

"Good ol' Sleuth!" he exclaimed, bending over to hug him. "Done trailed you out a panther!"

"Easy, Tommy," said Wash. "Remember he's tender."

"Good ol' dog! I sure be gentle. No mean ol' man goin' to hurt you no more."

Wash took his Appaloosa on toward the four horses staked across the glade. He had just stepped off when he caught a whiff of liquor, and he turned to find Mulholland an arm's length away. The rancher's face was puffed like a mad horned toad, and the veins in his temples seemed ready to pop.

"I'll take that dog of mine back now, Baker," Mulholland growled.

"You'll do what?"

"Sleuth. He's mine, and I'm takin' him back."

Mulholland turned and started away, but Wash seized his shoulder and spun him around. "What the hell you mean?"

"You got one of my dogs killed, so I'm takin' what's mine."

"Wasn't my fault what happened. You's the one kept sayin' 'shoot' when I couldn't see the thing."

Mulholland turned and yelled toward the campfire, where Tommy stood petting the old hound. "Sleuth! You's *my* dog. Get over here before I get my quirt!"

Everyone turned, including Sleuth, but the reactions that struck Wash most were the dog's abrupt cringe and Tommy's wide eyes.

Wash stepped around to face Mulholland again. "You already give me that dog."

"Thing cost me a bred heifer. I've got registration papers on him. Think I'd just up and give him away?"

"I've learned you can't predict what you'd do. I guess I'm still learnin'."

Mulholland shouted again for Sleuth. "I'll beat the hell out of you if you don't get over here!"

"Mr. Wash? Mr. Wash?"

Wash could hear Tommy's heartbreaking appeal and see the concern in his features as he knelt and embraced the hound protectively.

"Mulholland," said Wash, "you's not layin' another hand on that dog."

"You try and stop me."

Mulholland's saddle was on the snow under a pinyon near his staked sorrel, and Wash quickly secured the Appaloosa and followed him over. Bending over, the rancher took up his quirt, and when he stood up again, Wash was in his face.

"I asked you before what you wanted for him. I'll ask you again."

"Mean man! Mean man!" From across the clearing, Tommy was crying out, briefly drawing both men's attention.

"All right, Baker," Mulholland said smugly, "if you want the damned dog so bad, I'll tell you what I'll take for him."

"I'm listenin'."

Mulholland glanced again at Tommy. "That blazed-face

chestnut that clabber-head's so crazy about."

Wash could only stare into Mulholland's bloodshot eyes.

"Them's my terms," Mulholland added. "You don't like them, I'll take my dog and you can go to hell."

Wash could still hear Tommy's desperate petition, his angry cry. "Tommy's right," he said. "You *are* a mean son of a bitch."

Mulholland took a step toward Wash, and Wash took a step toward him, and matters that had been brewing since the Concho were ready to come to a head. Maybe they would have, but suddenly there was a voice from close behind.

"No!"

Wash turned and found Trey, the young man's nostrils flaring and hard lines bending the corners of his mouth. But Trey's glare wasn't for him; it was for Mulholland.

"You're not taking that dog, Father. The horse either."

"Stay out of this! If Baker wants that dog, he knows what it'll cost him!"

Trey stepped closer. "That chestnut is not his to trade. He gave it to Tommy. But you know that, don't you. You were right there when Mr. Baker did it."

"Get the hell out of my face, boy!"

"If ever a man spoke the truth, it's Tommy. You're a mean bastard and you always were."

Mulholland went into a rage and quirted him viciously—a shocking development between father and son—but when he tried it again, Trey tore the whip from his grasp so forcefully that Mulholland fell to the snow. He lay there, laboring for breath, seemingly too weak to rise, but Trey clearly had no interest in helping him.

"You want a horse for that dog?" demanded Trey as he stood over him. "All right, you've got one—that dun of mine soon as this hunt is over. I'm trading with you right now, and in turn I'm giving that dog to Mr. Baker."

Trey nodded to Wash and walked away with the quirt. Wash watched him all the way to the fire, where the young man allowed Tommy the privilege of throwing the whip in to burn.

CHAPTER TWELVE

Maybe it was the flask at his lips, or a false sense of superiority, or a childish need for payback.

Regardless, Wash wouldn't have thought that Mulholland had nerve enough to dominate the conversation after joining everyone at the fire. But there he was, standing across the flames from Wash and blathering away as nightfall brought a piercing cold.

"Bet all of you think it'll be safe sleepin' here by the fire. No such thing as safe when a grizzly's around."

Mulholland took a pull on the flask and went on.

"Knowed a old Frenchman, name of Baptiste, up in Colorado. He trapped there on Lost Creek west of Denver, the Front Range. Had the damnedest crooked neck you ever seen, all twisted over to his shoulder. I asked him, 'What in the hell happened to that neck of yours?' It was all scarred up, you know. 'Grizzly,' he tells me."

Mulholland may have been a blowhard, but Wash could tell by the faces in the firelight that the rancher had everyone's attention as he continued.

"He was sittin' by his campfire, mindin' his cookin', pitchblack out there behind him like it is here. First thing he knowed, a bear had him by the neck with his teeth."

"Mr. Wash? Mr. Wash?" appealed Tommy.

Wash was almost brushing shoulders with Tommy, but that didn't keep the worried man from grabbing Wash's arm and peering around into the dark.

"That's enough, Mulholland," said Wash.

Mulholland ignored him. "Paralyzed that trapper where he couldn't even holler. The thing started draggin' him off in the trees, and wasn't a thing in hell he could do about it."

"Mr. Wash! Mr. Wash!" exclaimed Tommy.

Wash glared at Mulholland. "I said, that's *enough*."

But the rancher seemed to be enjoying himself. "Yeah, hadn't been for somebody there with a gun, that grizzly would've had him a meal for sure. He—"

"Shut up! You hear me? Shut up!"

Stunned at Trey's outburst, Wash looked at the young man just beyond Tommy. Trey stood erect, his head tilted forward in confrontation and his knotted eyebrows overshadowing his eyes. Mulholland seemed to be as taken aback as everyone else, for he paled and the fire burned wider in his bloodshot orbs.

"Tommy doesn't want to hear it! Miss Grace either!" Trey continued.

"Just warnin' ever'body," said Mulholland.

"No! You just want to stir up panic! You're a cruel SOB"— Trey glanced left with a quick apology to Grace—"that abuses dogs and horses and, yeah, your own boy growing up!"

Wash had never seen Mulholland speechless before. When he did find quiet words, he was clearly subdued.

"You don't have to air our dirty laundry around ever'body."

Trey went quiet, and his father turned his back to the fire— the only way of hiding from everyone when there was no warm place to go.

"Let *them* kill it, Rosindo! Maybe it's dead! I want to go home!"

The roar they had heard earlier had alarmed Rosindo as much as Benita, but they had reclaimed the roan and continued on the trail without incident. Nevertheless, as Rosindo stared into their newly kindled fire and Benita pleaded from alongside, he was plagued by thoughts as dark as the night.

Ever since a gunshot had silenced the baying of dogs late in the day, Benita had again embraced the idea that *el oso plateado* might have fallen prey to the six riders who tracked it. Still, Rosindo had convinced himself that the report had come from behind rather than ahead, the direction in which the bear's spoor seemed to lead.

Now that they had made camp, however, under the thinning, red-and-gold foliage of a maple out of the gulch drainage, he wasn't so sure. After all, the gunshot had seemed to echo from everywhere. That's why he saw in the lapping flames so troubling a vision—their father wandering for eternity in a foredoomed search for the peace that Rosindo alone could have ensured.

"They killed it!" said Benita. "I know they killed it! Now we can start home, Rosindo!"

"You . . ." His voice didn't want to work as he considered the consequences if she was right. "You don't understand, my sister. It has to be *me*. The *curandero* said *me*."

"They killed it! I know they did! They—"

"No!" He spun and took her by the shoulders. "*El oso plateado* is still alive!"

"You're pinching me! You're pinching me!" she exclaimed.

He could see the surprise in her eyes, open to their fullest and reflecting firelight. Ashamed, he turned away, crushed by the burdens he carried. He had never mistreated his sister and he didn't know what had come over him, but he also knew the mission on which he had been sent.

The great bear was alive! For their *papá's* sake, it had to be!

And Rosindo wondered if there was anything he wouldn't do—including turning his rifle on someone—to discourage the six riders so that he could take the shot that would let him see his father in Heaven.

As Wash shivered in his bedroll, the frigid night seemed to hold danger unlike any he had faced since he had lain under a similarly uncaring sky on the Concho.

Between an insulating saddle blanket underneath and a tarp flush on top, he lay near the hissing fire, his head against the seat jockey of his saddle. Only his sleeved arms were exposed, a necessity to stay vigilant with his Colt Model 1878 shotgun. But vigilance had led to panic on that earlier night, and he silently swore at Mulholland for summoning out of the gloom all the ghosts that were bent on crushing the fragile hope that Wash had left in life.

But the impact of Mulholland's calculated efforts to alarm wasn't limited to Wash. As Wash had directed, Tommy had stretched out between him and the fire, a position that offered the greatest protection from an attacking grizzly. But even with Sleuth curled up beside him, Tommy stirred anxiously, whimpering in his sleep. From the rustle of tarps and blankets, others must have slept just as restlessly, and Wash wished that he had insisted that Grace unfurl her bedroll closer to him.

I'll kill him, Papa. When I grow up, I'll kill Ed Mulholland for you.

Like a thunderclap rolling out of the sky, Grace's long-ago words came to him, a devastating indictment of who Wash had become. She had made the statement again only this morning, and he seemed to hear it in the voices of both a child and an adult. All day long, he had dwelled on the matter, but he had never found an opportunity to discuss with her the vengeance he had recklessly planted in her mind.

Reckless, hell. It had been heinous to indoctrinate a malleable child that way, and he wondered if, at this very moment, she lay awake, plotting to fulfill the promise of a six-year-old.

If anyone needed killing, it was Mulholland, and Wash suspected that there was scarcely a person among them who didn't wish him dead. Tommy didn't have a mean bone in his body, but Wash knew that if the red-haired man could rid the world of one person to make things better for animals like Sleuth, the choice would be easy. Trey had even more reason, considering his upbringing and the scars he evidently still carried. Only Isom had not spoken ill of Mulholland, but the clergyman had witnessed his torture of Sleuth and his spiteful psychological abuse of Tommy in particular.

Maybe it would be Mulholland whom the grizzly would drag away by the neck.

The thought went with Wash into a sleep troubled by his long search for the peace that Emma continued to assure him could be his if only he believed.

Emma . . . Emma . . .

I want to believe again.

In dream he relived a summer day on the Lampasas when he had waded out thigh-deep, a nineteen-year-old in striped overalls and white shirt buttoned to the top under his suspenders. The mud on bottom oozed between his bare toes as a dark-suited older man, with gray chin whiskers and hair parted in middle, assumed a position beside him. Wash couldn't recall his name, but he could still feel the clergyman's hand on his back and see the witnesses beside the river.

They were all there: the women and girls with ankle-length dresses and bonnets, the young boys perched on pecan roots twisting out of the bank, the men in frock coats with hats reverently in their hands. The heat was oppressive, and women sheltered under broad umbrellas or stirred the air with homemade fans. Many congregants had hymnals, and as Wash waited with hands clasped penitently below his breast, he could hear the voices quietly proclaiming *"I once was lost, but now am found."*

"Keep your feet on bottom, brother," whispered the clergyman. Then the song ended, and he spoke loudly enough for everyone to hear.

"I baptize thee, Washington Baker, in the name of the Father, and of the Son, and of the Holy Ghost."

The clergyman's hand descended on Wash's face, blotting out the glare of the sun and all his misdeeds, and Wash responded to his guiding touch by lying back against the supporting hand between his shoulder blades. The warm water swept over Wash, symbolically cleansing him, and when he had come up, he had been a new man.

It had all been so real to him, a moment in time when he had shown by his actions to whom he belonged. For decades thereafter he had lived his life secure in who he was—and then had come a shotgun blast that had taken it all away from him.

Emma . . . Emma . . .

I want to believe again.

Wash awoke to the vicious barks of the bull terriers. He sat up quickly, his heart pounding and the shotgun ready as he spun left and right.

"What the hell!"

Mulholland's exclamation came from across the fire, but Wash had questions of his own as he scrambled to his feet. He couldn't see a thing, but the barks had given way to the terriers' snarls in the direction from which the grizzly had roared in daytime. Something was *there*, breaching the camp by dark, and he threw the butt of the shotgun against his shoulder and scanned the night.

Now the hounds bayed, a discord of noise that muffled any sounds of approach, and even in that instant of grave danger, Wash considered how the thunder had similarly diminished his senses on the Concho. It was reason enough to relax his thumb on the double hammers.

"Don't anybody shoot!" he warned.

Almost simultaneously, the dogs went quiet.

"Are we all here?" Wash asked. "Grace?"

"Yes, Papa."

"Trey?"

"Yes, sir."

"Brother Isom?"

"Here, Brother Baker."

"How about you, Tommy?" asked Wash.

There was no answer, and Wash spun to the blankets by the fire. Good God, had a bear dragged him away? "Tommy? Tommy, answer me!"

"Out here, Mr. Wash!" The reply came from out in the dark where the terriers had given warning.

Until Wash stepped across the bedding and took up a firebrand, he hadn't realized that Tommy and Sleuth were both gone.

"What the hell you doin' out there?" Wash demanded.

Sweeping the firebrand above his head, he went out into the gloom and saw a shadowy figure emerge.

"Just couldn't hold it in no more, Mr. Wash," said Tommy. "I taken ol' Sleuth to look after me good."

Wash's pulse raced more than ever, and he couldn't seem to find a breath. Following Tommy to the fire, he laid the shotgun across his tarp and tossed the firebrand into the coals. For a moment he stared down, trembling and remembering how he had twice looked down the barrels of his shotgun and scanned a dark night filled with threat. Then he whirled and seized Tommy by the shoulders.

"I could've shot you!" he cried. "Don't ever do that again!"

Wash turned and stalked away, not realizing until after the

Patrick Dearen

fact how violently he had shaken Tommy. But worse was the memory of Tommy's suddenly slack jaw and his stunned, wide eyes in the firelight.

CHAPTER THIRTEEN

The earsplitting crack of a rifle broke the stillness of the pre-dawn.

Shaken out of a deep sleep, Wash didn't know if he had dreamed it, but the report still rolled through the dark as he sat bolt upright and instinctively tightened his grip on the shotgun. Around him was bedlam, but there was nothing left of the campfire to light the scene.

More asleep than awake, he may have caught a whiff of gun smoke in the wind as he struggled to distinguish dream from reality. But the wild barking of the dogs was real enough, and so were the shadows moving against shadows and the voices that talked over one another. Nightmare or not, his first concern was for Tommy, and he spun in fear that he had wandered out in the night again and made himself a target.

"Tommy, you answer me right now!" he cried.

From alongside came a voice like the whimper of a scolded puppy. "Don't be mad no more, Mr. Wash. I . . . I stayed put like you say."

Wash didn't have time to feel guilty. "Grace, where are you?"

"I'm all right, Papa. Who shot?"

For the second time since nightfall, Wash called out to the others as he came to his feet. "Trey! Brother Isom! Mulholland!"

The first two answered quickly, while from across the fire ring came only a snort.

"That you over there, Mulholland?" demanded Wash.

"Damned stingin' lizard got me," the rancher grumbled.

The sting of a scorpion was like the brand of a hot iron, but Wash had more important concerns. "Who was it shot their rifle?"

With the dogs quieting down, there was only silence.

"Nobody?" pressed Wash.

"I think I'd dozed off, Papa," said Grace.

"I was in deep sleep, but seemed like it was right on top of us. Anybody awake at the time?"

When no one responded, Wash remembered what had happened in the canyon the day before. He was still dwelling on it when Trey spoke up.

"Must have been who we heard yesterday, Mr. Baker."

"I'm thinkin' that. But what would they be shootin' at? It's pitch-black still."

"Damn, that bite hurts," complained Mulholland. "Right under my short ribs."

Peering through the dark at Mulholland's shadow, Wash began to wonder. "First light's still a ways off. Let's get this fire built up so we can see a little."

Someone stirred the fire and exposed glowing coals, and once Wash added wood and blew gently, the smolder flared. Soon the flames threw a measure of light, and Wash turned to Mulholland. The rancher was on his feet and hiking up his coat and shirt, thereby baring his fleshy side to the campfire's flicker.

"What in the hell?" said Mulholland, passing his fingers along his skin. "Feels wet."

He held out his hand and twisted it, and when Wash shaded the glare of the fire and looked for himself, he saw what he half expected.

"Blood!" exclaimed Mulholland. "How—"

Wash went around the charred rocks and studied Mulholland's side from up close. Lighting still wasn't the best, but the shallow gash, an inch or two long in a roll of fat, was obvious enough.

"Damned if I know how I cut myself," said Mulholland.

"Take a look at your shirt and coat," said Wash.

"What for, Baker? No stingin' lizard done *this.*"

When Mulholland resisted, Wash assumed the initiative and reached for the bunched clothing under the rancher's elbow.

"Keep your damned hands to yourself!" Mulholland griped.

"Do it yourself then. Bet you find holes goin' in and comin' out. Same with your beddin'."

"Holes?" repeated Mulholland. "How come you to . . . ?"

He began to check, but Wash had more to say. "Wasn't no stingin' lizard, I'll grant you. It was a bullet."

At almost the same moment, Mulholland discovered it for himself.

"I-god! Rip in my shirt! A matchin' one in my coat!" He whirled to the woods left and right. "Who's takin' pot shots?"

Wash joined him in scanning the night. The dark hid all but the nearest pinyon limbs, but he was struck by the fact that among the entire party—Tommy, Trey, Isom, and Grace—only one failed to turn and look with them. It was as if that person knew that there was no reason to, and Wash shivered and edged nearer the fire in search of warmth that suddenly wasn't there.

"Couple of inches over and they'd've killed me!" said Mulholland.

Everyone was speaking now, but Wash couldn't hear. He was reliving too many things in the licking flames—for the person who hadn't looked was Grace.

"Mr. Wash? Mr. Wash?"

Tommy's voice broke through the memories.

"Somebody shoot mean man a-purpose?" Tommy added.

Wash's voice didn't want to work as he looked up from the

fire. "Stray bullet. That's all it was. Stray bullet from a hunter."

"But you say it be on top of us. You say 'What they be shootin' at, pitch-black and all?' "

For long seconds, Wash merely stared at the flash of the ever-changing firelight in Tommy's face.

"Rifle shot can go a . . . a awful long way," Wash finally succeeded in saying. "The report can sure carry too, way things echo."

Wash told him that, all right, and told everyone else as well. But mainly he tried to convince himself, for he was terrified that the promise of a six-year-old may have taken hold.

"Trey?" spoke up Mulholland.

Checking, Wash found the older rancher bathed in the glow of the flames.

"You hearin' all this, son?" Mulholland added. "Somebody went and shot me."

Trey, standing against the shadows across from Mulholland, turned away without a word.

"Step over and see about me, why don't you," said Mulholland.

Trey knelt and began rummaging through a saddlebag.

"Hell of a thing, me gettin' shot thataway," persisted Mulholland. "Come check on your old father."

Trey wouldn't look around.

"Hurtin' like hell, son," said Mulholland. "Sure wish you'd come here a minute."

But even as Mulholland virtually begged for the longest time, Trey stayed as unresponsive as if it were the wind that his father addressed.

As day broke cloudless and everyone prepared for the day's ride, Wash pondered that faint odor of gun smoke, real or dreamed.

Maybe too much time had passed to identify a recently fired rifle by sniffing the muzzle, but possibly he could twist a finger inside the barrel and detect powder residue. He casually sauntered about camp, looking and hoping, but he had an opportunity to check only Grace's weapon—and he chose not to, for he realized that he would rather not know.

And so he rode terrified by the prospect, as the hounds bayed from ahead and his horse plodded through snow that blinded under the glare of sunlight filtering through pinyons, junipers, and gray oaks. With the five other riders, he bore northeast, traversing rolling mountains broken by gentle canyons as the Appaloosa's hoofs grated the underlying rocks and the wind soughed through the swaying limbs. It was beautiful country, particularly with the contrast of the evergreen conifers against white, but Wash couldn't enjoy a moment of it.

He waited patiently for the party to string out, and then he pushed ahead to the right flank of Isom's bay so that he could speak privately.

"What you was sayin' yesterday." For a while, Wash heard only the rattle of riding tack and muffled drum of hoofs. "You was figurin' up what it'd take to get throwed in hell."

Isom neither responded nor gave him a glance.

Wash shuddered. "Awful place, the way you described it—cryin' and grindin' your teeth in a fire that just goes on and on. You really think it's that bad?"

Now Isom's head sank and he answered quietly, lifelessly. "Worse. It's worse, Brother Baker."

"Didn't think anything could be worse than bein' burned."

"Gehenna," said Isom. His voice began to quiver. "The valley of the sons of Hinnom. The trash pile outside the gates of Jerusalem. The fires burned day and night, never ending. The Lord used it to describe a place of suffering beyond what we're able to understand."

"I . . . I just can't imagine hellfire never endin'," Wash managed.

"It won't be fire, Brother Baker. It will be complete separation from the Almighty, from everything good. It will be worse than fire for those who deserve it."

Wash's shiver wouldn't go away, and he bunched his coat at his neck. "That's what I'm wonderin', who's got it comin' to them."

"All of us." Isom's cheek strangely began to glisten behind his steel-wire spectacles. "We're a generation of vipers who deserve the damnation of hell."

It was startling to hear a clergyman make such a blunt pronouncement, and it unsettled Wash.

"Then what chance we got?" he asked. "What chance *anybody* got?"

"That's sin, Brother Baker. It's a wall between us and the Almighty, a fortress high as these mountains."

"Can't nothin' get us over it? What's the use, then?"

Isom lifted his gaze to the sky and kept it there as a rivulet trickled down his face.

"*Sin!* It's *sin* that damns us!" Isom's chin began to quake, and when he looked down his voice became a whisper. "Confess it and . . . and ask the Lord's forgiveness, or . . . or it will be too late."

For long seconds, Wash rode in silence, trembling to an inner cold as he dwelled on so many things. Shaken as never before, he owned up to the two greatest misdeeds of his life.

"I've wronged both of my children," he said.

Isom slowed so that they rode squarely abreast and looked at him.

"I guess you know about my boy," Wash continued. "I guess your father told you about the drive. He wasn't no preacher man like you are, but he said the right words over his grave.

Not that it helped any."

The clergyman's eyes were fixed on him in an uncomfortable stare. "The Lord won't hold an accident against a man, Brother Baker. But woe unto him who speaks of good and commits evil, who puts darkness before light with a terrible, terrible deed."

"I . . . I wouldn't've done what I did for the world. Livin' with it all these years, I guess I got some idea what hell must be like."

Isom began to blink excessively and turned away. "The guilt . . . the pain . . . yes, hell."

Wash wished he hadn't burdened the clergyman.

"I'm sorry, Brother Isom. Never should've stirred up all the troubles you got yourself. The thing is, I done my girl wrong too, the notions I put in her head way back when she was little. Is . . . Is there anything too awful to be forgive for?"

When Isom hung his head again and his shoulders began to shake, Wash knew that the answer must be one that a man had to find for himself.

At sunset, a full moon would rise and seal their father's fate.

Desperate, Rosindo took up the trail at first light as Benita shivered at his back and ice crackled under the roan's hoofs. For miles they rode north and east through winding canyons and up slopes with gray oak and juniper. They skirted windy precipices and navigated mountainsides of sparkling rocks ready to slide. Down challenging slopes and across bottomland meadows, Rosindo forged on, unable to appreciate the stunning contrast of evergreens with the white of the quickly vanishing snow.

At the edge of a ponderosa-spangled meadow under a two-hundred-foot rock face, *el oso plateado*'s fading tracks turned back to the south-southwest up the drainage of a confined canyon. This course, too, was a snake track, either hugging a left-side cliff, three times the boy's height with a steep rise above, or veering to the right where lofty mountains showed in the distance through hackberry, buckeye, and mountain mahogany.

At a shallow pool mirroring bright sky, they climbed off to slake their thirst and let the horse water. For a couple of miles now, Rosindo had been unsure if they still followed the bear's spoor, for the melting snow had all but erased it and the roan's hoofs had tapped a cadence against underlying rock. Maybe the tracks were there, and maybe they weren't, and hope and wish were little to go on with so much at stake.

Rosindo's eyes began to sting.

He could no longer see. He was blind to his sister, kneeling and cupping water to her mouth. The reins were an afterthought, loose in his fingers as the roan shifted and drank. Only vaguely was he aware of the nearby cliff, the green of its draping fern standing out against the jagged face. Even more distant was any sense that behind the fern was a vertical crack, sizable and dark.

His *papá* was doomed, and there was nothing he could do.

Suddenly the horse jerked the reins from his hand and bolted. Whirling, Rosindo brushed his eyes in order to see through the emotion. Sixty yards up the gulch, at the limits of visibility through leafy sumac and red oaks and the stripped limbs of ash and bigtooth maples, something was rising to its feet—a furry, brown form, grizzled at the shoulders, too hulking to be a man. It must have stood eight feet, and as it threw its nose to the air and made a half circle with its head, the thing seemed to fix all its senses on Rosindo.

"*El oso plateado!*"

At the same moment that Rosindo cried out, the bear dropped to all fours, disappearing behind the flimsy underbrush that alone lay between the children and their father's killer.

"Rosindo! Rosindo!" cried Benita.

"He's smelled us!"

He spun in search of the roan but the horse was nowhere in sight, while the brush stirred on a line from where the bear had stood. The thrashing grew nearer by the second, the snapping of limbs chilling him as he seized his sister's hand.

"*Vaya con prisa!* Run, Benita, run!"

With no nearby trees stout enough to climb, he dragged her toward the cliff and the black fissure his subconscious told him was there. Half-hidden in the green fern that clung to the frosted rock, the zigzag cleft split the face from top to bottom. He lost a sandal as he ran, but he frantically stumbled on with Benita in tow.

He risked a glance back at the whipping underbrush and flopped face first, but scrambled up to his sister's cries and suddenly was there, the fern in his brow. The crack beyond was just wide enough to admit small shoulders, and the inner dark with its musty smell suggested depth.

"Inside!" yelled Rosindo. "Quick, Benita, quick!"

When she turned to him for an instant, she must have seen what was behind him, for she paled and her pupils went almost as wide as her full eyes. Then he shoved her inside and tried to follow, inching sideways between rock that gnawed at his back and chest even through his serapes.

He couldn't fit! The great bear was on him, and he couldn't fit!

But when a roar from behind shook the rock, he found motivation to squeeze through no matter how much hide he lost. He managed two short steps, and then three, and when something sharp and powerful grazed his shoulder from behind, he pushed farther with strength he didn't know he had and bumped his sister.

"Go back!" he shouted.

"I can't!"

"Go back!"

"There's no room!"

The fissure had widened here, just enough for Rosindo to turn and see the last thing he wanted: a massive shadow blotting out the jagged streak of daylight.

"He's going to get us!" said Benita. "Rosindo, he—"

But Rosindo heard no more, for a thrusting paw wider than his face clawed at him, coming so close that he could feel the stirring air.

With a cry, the muchacho pressed back, but there was no place to go. The great bear threw itself against the entrance and the claws came at him again, five four-inch knives trying to slash. Rosindo dodged and twisted, escaping by a hair's breadth only to face another lunge and another. When the paw withdrew, he thought that they had survived, but the moment became even more hopeless when the grizzly began clawing at the entrance.

"He's digging it out!" the muchacho shouted.

"Rosindo! Rosindo! Rosindo!"

Facing certain death, Rosindo remembered why he was here. His father's killer was barely more than an arm's length away, and while the *muchacho* and his sister would meet an end as horrible as their *papá's*, theirs would be a transition that would take them to Heaven. But to die this way, their mission unfulfilled, would forever deny their father the peace he deserved. He would be doomed to wander, a spirit never at peace, all because Rosindo had failed.

No! He wouldn't let it happen!

He reached under his serapes for the very knife with which he had skinned *el oso plateado's* smaller relative in the Fronterizas. For the love of his *papá,* and that of Benita, Rosindo would sell his life in the hope that the knife would sink home—a puny boy and a puny weapon, driven by something stronger than even the great silver bear.

The claws came at him again, but now the muchacho met them with a swishing blade. He missed and then struck, a slicing sweep with all the force he could muster. The bear roared in pain and the paw pulled back, only to lunge at him again. Once more, Rosindo's knife caught it hard, this time to the clack of steel against claws. Again *el oso plateado* bawled and withdrew, and for a second time the muchacho hoped the attack was over.

But hope wasn't enough, for yet again the silver bear began to rip away at the entrance with claws that could disembowel.

"Make it leave, Rosindo!" said Benita. "Make it leave!"

Rosindo wished there was a way, but he could only watch with ever-growing terror as dirt and rocks flew from the entrance. He could feel the grit and taste the dust as he trembled and waited, knowing what was to come. Once inside, *el oso plateado* would extend its forelimb and find them with its claws—terrible, raking things that, before killing, would shred his face and then Benita's. In this tight place, Rosindo would have no chance to get inside the forelimbs and clinch with the bear under its powerful jaws, the only position from which he could try to drive the knife into its heart.

But the act of digging must have been painful, for *el oso plateado* paused and snapped its jaws alongside its wounded paw. As the muchacho searched for the courage to go outside and face his *papá*'s killer, the bear moved away from the entrance. How far, Rosindo couldn't tell.

"Is it gone?" asked his sister. "Tell me it's gone! Tell me, Rosindo!"

Knowing this might be their last moment together, he reached back and found her hand. "Stay here and I'll come back for you. If I don't . . ." His voice choked. "No matter what you hear, *stay where you are.*"

"What do you mean, my brother?"

He squeezed her fingers. "Promise me! Wait all day if you have to. When you come out, cover your eyes until you're up on the bank. When you get there, look for horse tracks."

"Why are you telling me this?" she asked.

But Rosindo suspected that she already knew. "The tracks will take you to the roan, and you'll be all right."

"No, Rosindo! No!"

"Promise me!"

The only response was a sob, and he slipped from her grasp and edged toward the daylight and whatever fate it held for him.

CHAPTER FOURTEEN

"Mr. Wash awful mad at me, Little Miss."

The mid-morning sun was melting the snow. It dropped in clumps from pinyons and alligator junipers, and the stiff, glazed limbs of gray oaks that earlier had crackled to the brush of Grace's horse were now thawed and pliable. Where the rays broke through and struck the slope flush, bare ground appeared in patches, and as her roan crossed this gentle stretch that dropped to the left, its hoofs momentarily clomped across wet bedrock.

Troubled by whatever had come between Trey and her, Grace rode tired-eyed at the hindquarter of Tommy's dapple gray and a nose ahead of Isom's bay, the three of them separated from the others in the party. Mulholland and Trey were out of view ahead, nearer the baying hounds, while an hour ago Wash had dropped back without a word and was somewhere behind Isom. But while Grace's father may have been out of sight, he was very much on Tommy's mind.

"He ain't never yelled at me before," Tommy added as he faced her. "He ain't never grabbed a-hold of me."

"He was just worried about you," consoled Grace. "I think he nearly shot you, same as he did Joe."

It slipped out unexpectedly, a topic long forbidden.

Tommy jerked his head back and puckered his mouth. "Oh my gosh! Oh my gosh! You *know*, Little Miss! Oh my gosh! Oh my gosh!"

His look of surprise became one of distress, and Grace moved quickly to calm him. "It's all right, Tommy."

"Mr. Wash tell me once, 'Don't never talk about it, Tommy! Don't say nothin' to Little Miss. Somethin' that bad, she don't need to know!' "

"I'm old enough now, but it's still awful hard on Papa. I think the grizzly we're after has stirred up all the bad memories. That's why he reacted like he did when you came out of the dark."

"Poor Mr. Wash," Tommy said with childlike compassion. "Poor Mr. Wash, thinkin' his own boy Mr. Grizzly."

"The arrogance," Isom spoke up quietly. "The arrogance, to think we can hunt down this bear."

Grace turned in the saddle.

"We can't, preacher Isom?" asked Tommy.

"It's after *us,*" said Isom. "From the start—it's been after *us.*"

Now Grace was confused. "I've got questions too, Brother Isom. What do you—?"

"Jehovah set the grizzly on us to bare what we've done." Abruptly, Isom's preaching voice dominated. "Our hands are defiled with blood, our fingers with iniquity. Our lips have spoken lies, our tongues have muttered perverseness. The bear's lying in wait to deliver Jehovah's judgment."

"What is it I done wrong?" Tommy asked in alarm. "I don't want no bear draggin' me off!"

" 'Woe to them that devise iniquity, and work evil upon their beds,' " quoted the clergyman.

"You're scaring Tommy, Brother Isom," interjected Grace. Then she faced the dapple gray and tried to change the subject. "Tommy, Papa said Sleuth treed that panther like he was a young dog again. You're sure taking good care of him."

Tommy nervously scanned the brush. "Mean man say a grizzly up and grabbed that trapper by the neck!" Protecting himself, he scrunched his shoulders and kept up his vigilance.

"So tell me, Tommy," she persisted. "What are you going to call that blazed-face chestnut? Have you picked out a name yet?"

He looked at her and seemed on the verge of calming, but Isom wouldn't leave the matter alone.

"The children mocked Elisha," recounted the clergyman, "and Jehovah sent two she bears down and tore them limb from limb."

When Grace turned again to Isom and called his name, no one seemed at home behind his steel-wire spectacles.

"Please, Brother Isom," she implored. "You're frightening us just like Mr. Mulholland."

The mention of the rancher clearly provoked something in the preacher.

"Edward Mulholland—the hypocrite!" Isom lifted his gaze beyond Grace, as though he could see Mulholland through the concealing brush. "You sit with the trustees of the camp meeting, but you're like a sepulcher, white on the outside but full of a dead man's bones. Do we think we can mock the Lord with our evil?"

Grace didn't know, but as she considered the pledge of the young girl who still lived inside her, there was something gravely concerning in what he said.

Outside the fissure, a man-killer was about, and with Rosindo's every step in the slush, he expected the wounded bear to charge out of the woods.

But the limbs of nearby hackberry and mahogany remained still, and the yellow foliage of black cherries barely fluttered in a breeze. Up and down the gulch, leafy sumac and red oaks seemed calm, and the defoliated limbs of bigtooth maple and ash rested in place.

Maybe *el oso plateado* had left, or maybe it was still there, ready to swoop down with frightening speed. If only he had his carbine! The skinning knife in his hand was utterly inadequate, a last gasp measure against the very manifestation of *el diablo* that had killed his father, and yet the muchacho clutched the bone handle tightly and pressed ahead.

He found his huarache and strapped it on. At first, he saw no sign of the roan, and then up the gulch he glimpsed what could have been a horse disappearing around a bend. He took a few steps in its direction, for he knew that if the roan strayed too far with the rifle and supplies, he might never find it. Abruptly, he noticed a drip trail of blood marking the drainage, and when he stopped and glanced over his shoulder, he could trace it back to the fissure.

Wounded by the knife, *el oso plateado* had gone this way.

Shivering to the cold and more, Rosindo knew that he and Benita could die unless he recovered the roan. And yet to do so, he would march straight into the domain of something that could kill even more surely.

With a look back at the fissure, the muchacho did what he must. But with each cautious pace up the canyon, every hammer of his heart, he anticipated and planned for the worst. He would not lure *el oso plateado* back to Benita's hiding place; he would flee toward the hackberries and mahoganies on the right or the fifteen-foot cliff on his left. And when all else failed, he would turn his knife on their father's killer and die in the knowledge that he had done all he could.

Rosindo advanced around the first bend, and the straightaway ahead was empty. He negotiated a second crook, and the blood spoor still continued on under the wall of rugged rock. Then he brushed around an outcrop on the left, and his luck ran out.

Fifty yards ahead, grim against a serene stretch of snow and bedrock, reared *el oso plateado*.

The beast must not have seen him, for the back of the silver-tipped shoulder hump was to the boy. But the way the nose searched the air as the head turned made it almost certain that the bear had caught his scent, and Rosindo shrank behind the outcrop and threw his back against the cold rock.

Madre de Dios!

He had seen the bear's quickness and knew that he had only seconds. Whirling, he checked the cliff at his brow and saw that it sprang up to a shrubby slope a dozen feet above. The pitch was nearly vertical, but the face was as wrinkled as the old *curandero's* features, and Rosindo put away the knife and desperately began to climb.

Kicking and clawing, he managed eighteen inches and then three feet more, flakes of displaced rock flying as he dug with his fingers. He seemed to ascend at the pace of *tortuga,* the turtle, while *el oso plateado* had to be barreling toward him like a runaway horse. Any moment the rake-like claws would seize him and drag him down, and he wouldn't even be able to draw his knife.

Jesucristo! Help me!

He searched blindly for toe holds that weren't there, and just as he was certain that the grizzly lunged for him, he gripped the rim above and scrambled over the edge. Sprawled breathless under a dwarf oak in talus impossible to climb, he suddenly heard the bear slap at the cliff, and slap again.

It was coming up after him!

Trapped, he reached for his knife and twisted around to face the killer. But even as he looked down, he realized that what he heard was the pound of his own pulse in his ears.

El oso plateado wasn't there.

Rosindo stood, weak in the aftermath of his panic. Now that he was out of the canyon's muffling depths, he heard the faint baying of hounds. He couldn't pinpoint their location, but his scan up and down the gulch revealed that the grizzly had moved on. Maybe it had never scented Rosindo. Regardless, the mucha- cho was alive—and struck by what he saw through the limbs of red oak, ash, and bigtooth maples across the drainage.

His horse.

A descent was always more treacherous than a climb up, and just as Rosindo started down, he slipped and plunged. He was sure that he could break his fall with his feet and hands, but he tumbled off balance and the sheer rock of the streambed surged up with crushing force.

Dazed, he was abruptly back at a grave in the Fronterizas. His father's *bulto* was there, motioning again and again. *Sí,* out of a full moon, *el oso plateado* was rising up, a terrifying presence guarding the way to Heaven.

And all Rosindo could do was stare and weep and know that he had failed.

CHAPTER FIFTEEN

Wash's ride through fear grew darker.

With a brief exchange with Grace and a hard look at the .30-30 in her saddle scabbard, he passed her and pushed ahead. He had lagged to dwell on his failures, and had she been alone, he might have summoned his courage for a talk that he figured no father had ever had with a daughter.

That trace of gun smoke, so fleeting in the pre-dawn, seemed stronger than ever, at least in reflection.

It continued to dominate even after he left Grace far behind and fell in behind Trey as the young man's dun sloshed along a snowy mountainside that rose sharply on the right. Except for a glance back and a nod, Trey seemed no more inclined to talk than Wash, and for a while they rode in silence to the baying of the hounds. Somewhere ahead and above, Sleuth's throaty bark was easily identifiable, but as Wash studied the sparsely wooded slope and rocky rim five hundred feet up, he couldn't pinpoint the location. Sleuth may have been past his prime, but the eagerness in his cry told Wash that the poor thing lived life to the fullest again, now that Mulholland was out of the picture.

"I appreciate you steppin' in the way you did about that old dog," said Wash.

"Yes, sir," Trey said without turning.

"But it's not right for my differences with your father to get you caught in the middle."

For a while, neither spoke as the horses nodded along to the

153

protest of saddle leather.

"Our strife's got nothing to do with you, Mr. Baker," said Trey. "It goes back far as I can remember."

The disclosure saddened Wash; he couldn't image a father and son never being close, even if they were Mulhollands. He didn't know how to respond, so he said nothing.

Trey continued. "Growing up, you don't know how much I envied your relationship with . . . with Joe."

He had difficulty speaking Joe's name, but Wash abruptly found his own voice just as reluctant.

"Don't guess I . . . I ever knew that."

"There was always so much respect between the two of you," said Trey. "You corrected him when he needed it; I guess everybody needs straightening out every now and then. But you could be firm without being cruel. Patient, too, instead of overbearing.

"Take that drive we were all on. You took a couple of wet-behind-the-ears boys under your wing. You did your best to make hands out of us, when all we cared about was which one of us threw the best shadow with those big hats of ours."

"We was all young once," said Wash. "Figure ever'body deserves a chance."

For a brief moment, Trey went quiet, as if pondering. "Yes, sir, I'd've traded places in a heartbeat with . . . with . . ."

This time, Joe's name just wouldn't come, and an uncomfortable silence ensued before Wash found words.

"For better or worse, I guess, all we can do is play the hand we's dealt." He gave a long sigh that seemed to drain his strength. "I was dealt a pretty tough one on that drive."

Just shy of a house-sized boulder mottled with orange and green lichen, Trey drew rein, and when he twisted about, his face was wrenched by emotion.

"Mr. Baker, I want you to know—the wrong boy died that night."

Trey clearly had more to say, but all Wash could do was wait and stare, struck by the moist eyes, the splotched complexion, the tremoring jaw. Twice the young man started to speak, but not until his third try did painful words begin to come.

"That whole trip, we were always daring each other, me and . . . me and Joe. One time, it'd be him daring me to have an outlaw bronc roped out for the morning. The next, it'd be me daring him to violate one of the cook's rules. Maybe ride in from upwind and throw a big dust over the fire, or tie his horse to the chuck wagon. We went back and forth that way all the time, just a couple of boys who didn't know any better. We never dreamed we'd get anybody hurt.

"Then came that night when the storm blew in. 'A grizzly,' Father said. 'Not another man-killer like it to be found. Eight hundred pounds, claws long as your fingers, jaws wide enough to crush a man's skull.' While he was panicking everybody, you were making sure we were all safe around the wagon.

" 'Pitch-black out there, except for lightning,' you told us all. 'Don't go off from camp unless it's a case of have-to. If anybody sees something, issue a challenge before you shoot. And for God's sake, if you're the one challenged, answer loud and quick.' You told us, Mr. Baker, you told us all, and then—"

From beyond the concealing boulder came a sudden shout—something about the dogs and bear high on the mountain. It was an outburst punctuated by the kind of swearing that only Mulholland could do, and Trey straightened in the saddle and gigged the dun ahead. Wash followed, and forty yards past the boulder they came upon Mulholland's sorrel tied to a gnarled pinyon.

From the lower reaches of the steep pitch above, Mulholland continued to spew profanity as he struggled up, his .30-40 glinting in the rays. He had unleased the bull terriers, a sign that the quarry was near, and from much higher on the mountain their barks mixed with the bays of the hounds. Once more, Mulholland yelled something about the grizzly, and as Wash swung off the Appaloosa and drew the Colt Model 1878 from its boot, he girded himself for the righteous shotgun blast that had eluded him through all the years of regret.

At Trey's underslung boot heels, he started up, bad knee and all, his free hand down on the slope for balance. Wash had never known so much snow to fall in these mountains, but he also had never known snow to melt so quickly. It was slush with an icy base, and he slipped and slid all the way, accomplishing three steps only to lose two. Where Trey and Mulholland, and the dogs before them, hadn't obliterated the trail, he could make out a spoor that had to be the grizzly's. But the latter tracks were exaggerated and ill-defined, the snow not firm enough to hold a shape.

Wash and Trey gained steadily on Mulholland, and by time they overtook him, the contours of the mountain muted the cries of the hidden dogs.

"What you got, Mulholland?" asked Wash. The rancher had paused at a small boulder to huff with his head down.

"Damn!" For several heaves of his lungs, it was all that Mulholland could manage. "Ever' time I look up, I go lightheaded."

"Bear up there?"

"What the hell kind of question's that?" Mulholland sucked air again. "Think I'm climbin' this for the fun of it?"

Wash was breathless as well. "Stay here if you's not up to it."

"Like hell. A cattle killer up there. I seen what happens when you do the shootin'."

Meanwhile, Trey had passed Mulholland, and the older man called after him. "Could use a hand here, son!"

Trey's boots continued to dig into snow.

"Side's dealin' me misery where I got shot!" Mulholland added.

But Trey pulled away without a word, and Mulholland pushed on unaided, grunting and swearing more. Wash followed, tracing the rancher's shadow as wetness worked through the stitching of his boots. The days of acclimation may have helped, but Wash wondered if Mulholland could make this ascent any better than he had on Sawtooth. Twice the rancher fell facedown in the snow, and the second time that he did, he lay imploring Wash with an outstretched arm.

"Won't nobody help me?" he gasped. "Me all shot and bleedin'?"

But Wash had heard a greater call, and he had no intentions of surrendering it. He brushed past the sprawled man and set his sights on Trey forty yards above, and beyond on a band of dark rock stark against the snow. Trey worked his way up through it and disappeared, and by the time Wash navigated the same brief chute and could see him again, the five dogs seemed to bark in place just above a final colonnade of rock against the blue of the sky.

"They've got him cornered!" he shouted at Trey. "Wait for me! I need to take the shot!"

The young man ascended a couple of steps more before looking back.

"You hear me?" asked Wash. "Give me the shot!"

Trey raised an arm in acknowledgment and continued to climb.

Wash's laboring chest seemed on fire from the cold air, but he grimly fought on, driven by anticipation. In the shade of the fifteen-foot rock columns, the snow grew firmer, and he burst up through a windy breach and abruptly was on the summit, a tortured man shouldering his shotgun in hope of redemption.

Over the rising barrel, glinting in the sun, he saw Trey on the right, his rifle loose at his side. Too, he saw the baying hounds and growling bull terriers, the five of them in a frenzy under a mature, twelve-foot ponderosa with its top shorn as if by lightning. The thick trunk had a slight lean, and the terriers were leaping at the red bark, vainly trying to gain the broken limb near top.

There, perched just out of reach and calmly looking down as the wind stirred its coat, was a bear.

A black bear.

It was a sizable one, a three-hundred-pound sow that, had it been on all fours, might have stood three feet high at the shoulder and stretched five feet. Shining in the sun, its fur could have been mistaken at a distance for a white-tipped grizzly's. But unlike a grizzly, a black bear had no shoulder hump, and the profile of its face was straight rather than sunken. Nor were its paws as massive, and its retractable claws were less than half as long.

Maybe this bear paled in comparison to its grizzled cousin, but it was still a formidable animal, and Wash would have hated to get caught between a black bear of any size and its cubs.

"*Grizzly*," he said, shaking his head. "Your father needs to see this, the way he was hollerin'."

"Some people," said Trey, "could stand correcting in lots of ways."

As they waited, Wash wanted to hear what else Trey had to say about that night in '80, but with the hounds and bull terriers in an uproar, this wasn't the time to ask. Nevertheless, as the minutes passed, what remained unspoken grew so powerful that Wash could no longer hear the dogs—not when thunder blared in his memory and he challenged again and again the thing coming at him in the dark.

Finally Mulholland came wheezing up between the rock columns. Collapsing on hands and knees at the summit, he drew Wash back into the present.

"There's your grizzly, Mulholland," said Wash, motioning to the ponderosa.

Looking up, the flushed rancher squinted and tried to speak. When he couldn't find breath enough, he lowered his head again.

"Trey . . . son . . ." For a while, he was too winded to say more. "Things go black 'less I keep my head down."

Wash had no sympathy. "Want me to tell you what you was chasin' after?"

But Mulholland evidently had seen well enough to make out the bear. "Told you yesterday, took a damned limb in my eye." With difficulty, he came to his feet and stumbled closer. "You dogs shut up and you can wool the thing in a minute."

But the bull terriers and hounds were too overcome by excitement. The brindle terrier continued to leap at the ponderosa, and so did the white terrier with black around its ears. Even the female bloodhound, so prized by Mulholland for its tracking skills, was caught up in the mania, and it threw itself again and again at the angling tree. Just as the rancher neared, the female's momentum took it a full seven or eight feet up, and when the small hound slid down, it lost its balance and sprawled between bull terriers ready to maul the first thing that fell.

It was a terrible sight, two dogs bred for battle attacking the gentle hound. Whenever Mulholland had fed the terriers, only the pop of his whip had kept the pair from fighting, and Wash spun in search of something to subdue the dogs. He took up a three-foot limb, but when he turned again, he found a swearing Mulholland wading into the fray.

"Let her alone!" Mulholland bellowed at the bull terriers. "Best dog I got!"

Suddenly the rancher went down and the crazed terriers were all over him, snarling and snapping with their powerful jaws.

"Get the hell off of me!"

As he kicked and fought back, his shouts turned into cries for help, for the law of blood sports had seized the terriers. The stronger would survive only at the expense of the weaker, and the bloodlust bred into the dogs through generations overwhelmed any deference to Mulholland as pack leader. Canine teeth flashed and struck, a frightful mauling that drew Wash and his limb into the conflict. Unable to club the terriers without hitting Mulholland, he could only stab and try to drive a wedge between the dogs and rancher.

It seemed hopeless, and then a rifle boomed in Wash's ears and something large and black streaked down through his vision. When it slammed to the ground mere feet away, he could feel the impact through his boots.

Startled, Wash pulled away, an instinctive action that may have spared him, for the gunshot bear was still very much alive. The bear turned on the five dogs with a roar, a wounded animal slapping left and right as it contended for its life. The game terriers, no longer interested in Mulholland, launched a counterattack, one gripping the bear by the ear while the other lunged for the throat under the yawning jaws.

Mulholland rolled to his shoulder, but he was still dangerously close to the fight, and the moment he looked up, Wash gripped his outstretched hand. If there was anyone Wash could never have imagined rescuing from a bear, Mulholland was the man, but he quickly dragged the rancher out of harm's way.

The bear was bleeding from the gunshot and losing strength fast, a circumstance the bull terriers seemed to sense. They redoubled their assault, but the brindle terrier sacrificed caution in its aggressiveness, and the bear used its forepaws to draw the dog to its mouth and clamped its jaws across the neck. Shaking the dog violently, the bear had one less terrier to fight, but the act took the last of the bear's strength, and soon Sleuth and a second hound joined the white-and-black terrier in mauling the dead animal.

Mulholland writhed in the snow. He had puncture wounds on his hands, and blood seeped through tears in his duck trousers. The dogs had ripped several buttons from his coat and had shredded the sleeves, but the heavy wool had saved him from greater injury. He was ashen and clearly shaken, but he still had the awareness to unleash a torrent of invectives against the terriers as he sat up.

Wash turned to Trey. "That was smart thinkin', shootin' that bear down. Dogs was eatin' your father alive."

The young man leaned his rifle against the ponderosa. "I made sure I only wounded it. I wanted it to have some fight left."

"Sure drawed those terriers away." Then Wash faced the lacerated man who struggled to his feet. "I'd say you was pretty lucky, Mulholland."

"Lucky, hell! I'm chewed up! Look at my hands!" Reaching down, Mulholland winced as he snatched up his .30-40. Then his voice softened. "Trey . . . son . . . ? Come see about me, won't you?"

But Trey had walked away to check the female hound, which lay mangled and bleeding. The dog turned its baggy eyes toward him and whined, and moments after the young man placed a compassionate hand on its wrinkled head, the animal convulsed and went still.

Turning his attention to the bear carcass, Trey pulled a skinning knife and opened the underbelly so that the viscera were exposed. Obviously concerned that the terrier would never allow Sleuth and the second bloodhound to eat, he disemboweled the carcass and tossed a sizable portion aside.

"Yours," he told the eager hounds.

As soon as Trey stepped away, Wash flinched to another rifle blast that threw the bull terrier up against the bear's wind-ruffled fur—a third animal to bloody the snow and die. Wash whirled, his ears buzzing and acrid gun smoke singeing his nostrils as Mulholland lowered the .30-40 with an oath.

"When a man's own stuff turns on him . . ." said Mulholland. Then he looked at Trey. "Son, help me down the mountain, would you? Could you do that for your old father?"

But Trey merely took up his Winchester and started down alone.

Chapter Sixteen

Rosindo was cold and wet, and when he opened his eyes, he understood why.

He sprawled with his cheek flush against rock, and away from him unfurled the sky, reflected in water an inch or so deep. Soaked and shivering, he sat up and got his bearings. The cliff rose up at his shoulder, and the slush that had covered the streambed had fully melted. He seemed all right, except for a knot above his ear, but he must have lain here a long time.

Rosindo stood, a little groggily, and looked up and down the drainage. There was no sign of the great bear, not even a drip trail of blood, for the thin layer of water across the bedrock had dispersed it. He sloshed across to the far bank where he had seen the roan from the rim of the cliff. He didn't expect to find the horse still there, but when he broke through a tangle of ash, bigtooth maple, and red oak, the sight of the roan grazing on bunched sideoats grama lifted his spirits.

Maybe, just maybe, he could still track down *el oso plateado* before it was too late.

He wasted no time retrieving the horse, but even before he swung astride, he untied the rifle and made sure it was ready to fire. Turning the roan into the streambed where passage would be easier, he splashed the animal down the gulch and soon drew rein before the black fissure.

"Benita! It's all right. Come out!"

The only reply was the hollow play of his own voice inside.

Rosindo called again, and when there was still no answer, he began to panic. With carbine in hand, he frantically dismounted. Clinging to the reins, he shouted her name and rushed to the black zigzag behind the fern's draping greenery. The opening seemed wider than before, or was it his imagination? The freshly broken rock looked brighter, stripped of its patina inside to the length of the great bear's forelimb, and the crevice floor was littered with debris—and something more.

In terror, Rosindo secured the horse to a jag of rock in the cliff and edged through, not wanting to see but knowing he must. There was no room to bend down, but he worked his foot underneath the foreign article and brought it high enough to snatch.

A serape.

One of Benita's serapes.

No!

Yelling her name, he pushed through the dark, the close-set walls punishing with every inch. Only when he struck solid rock in the farthest reaches did the passage widen, and he turned in disbelief to the jagged light at the entrance and sank to the floor, the coarse wall chafing his spine. For a moment he wallowed in despair, and then he dragged himself up and worked his way outside.

He spun left and right, his shouts carrying up and down the gulch. Here, too, shallow water spread across the bedrock, and the blood trail had disappeared with the slush. He ran to the far bank and called her name again, and when she didn't answer, he fired two quick shots in the air and listened, hoping against hope that she would respond.

But no reply came, and when he couldn't find tracks among the clumps of grama, he stared at the serape in his hand and faced a truth too awful to accept.

★ ★ ★ ★ ★

"Are you not feeling well, Miss Grace?"

Grace supposed that her body language on the roan was a giveaway as she rode a little ahead of Trey, the two of them apart from the others along a slope with gray oaks and junipers underneath a lofty colonnade on the right. She hadn't realized that she slumped and gazed down at the saddle horn, nor was she aware that she quaked to her quiet weeping. When Trey called her attention to her bearing, she dabbed at her eye, but her reply all but hung in her throat.

"I . . . I wasn't sure you cared anymore," she murmured.

For a while, only the muffled hoofbeats in slush broke the silence, and when Trey did respond, his voice was subdued.

"I guess I can understand why you'd think that."

Grace straightened a little, expecting him to offer an explanation. When none came, her shoulders bent again, and Trey must have noticed.

"You deserve somebody better," he said. "You, especially."

Grace looked back, but he averted his eyes, leaving her to focus on the thin, red scab and ugly bruise above his brow.

"What's that mean, Trey? You're the best—"

"You don't know me, who I am, what . . . what I did."

"I know you're good to me. You're good to Tommy and you're good to dogs, and you stand up for all of us when your . . ."

Your father, she started to say, but she decided that nothing beneficial could come from reminding him of his upbringing. What was it Papa had said? That a person can always tell the kind of calves he'll get by the bull he runs?

She drew rein, forcing Trey to do the same. Pivoting in the saddle, she was hurt even more because he chose to stare down past his dun's breast rather than face her.

"I . . . I can't go on like this," she sobbed. "I barely sleep anymore. I can't eat. All I think about is what could've happened for you not to want to be around me anymore."

"It's not you, Miss Grace. It's me. All of it, just me. My do-ing, my fault."

"Can't . . . Can't you even look at me? Do you hate me that much?"

For days Trey had refused to make eye contact, even as she had placed herself before him and pleaded. But now her words reached a part of him where all else had failed, for he lifted his head and his blue eyes fixed on her.

"How could you think that of me, Miss Grace?" he asked. "Hate? Don't you know I love y—"

He tried to catch himself, but it was too late, for pent-up emotion flooded her. She could feel the wetness squeeze out between her eyelids as it refracted the sunlight and distorted his features.

He wagged his head as if in self-loathing. "I'm sorry. I never meant to say that. I wasn't ever going to say that. I wouldn't have trifled with you for anything, you of all people, knowing it couldn't work. I . . . I'm just . . . sorry."

Grace had never been so uplifted and dispirited in the same moment. "Why wouldn't it work, Trey? I love you too!"

Once more, he avoided her eyes. "You wouldn't if you knew."

"Knew what? What is it that's bothering you so!"

He seemed to have to use all his willpower to face her again, and there was sheer sadness in the way his raised eyebrows came together.

"Why do you have to look so much like him?" he asked.

"Like who?"

When his chest rose and fell, he no longer seemed to have the strength or will to stay upright in the saddle. "Like . . . like Joe."

"That's what you started to ask the other night, wasn't it? What could Joe have to do with us?"

"I'll tell you the same thing I told your father this morning." A tiny stream trickled down his face. "The wrong boy died that night."

"The wrong—?"

"Every time I look at you, I see him. Don't you understand, Miss Grace?"

She didn't, but whatever he held inside showed in his contorted features.

"I see the boy I got killed," Trey went on, his voice choking. "I see the best friend I ever had, and the lightning is flashing and he's there next to me on the ground and your father's lifting him up and crying his name over and over again. My friend, my best friend, dead because of me, all because of *me*."

Grace's emotions were as unchecked as his. "I still can't understand! You've got to help me understand! You weren't like this before, not till the hunt started!"

"It brought it all back. All these years, I buried it, but all the talk about the grizzly brought it back."

He was about to say more, but abruptly a voice rose up from the way they had come, back past an alligator juniper with spidery dead limbs jutting from its greenery.

"Little Trey! Little Trey!"

Trey turned, and between his spiritless figure and the juniper appeared a dapple gray with Tommy in the stirrups. As usual, his floppy hat was askew and his unkempt red hair dangled across his freckled face.

"Little Trey! Little Trey!" he said as he reined up breathless at the hindquarter of Trey's dun.

"I'm here, Tommy."

"Pappy of yours a-callin' you, Little Trey! Preacher Isom say so. 'Run get Little Trey,' he tells me. Says he's tired of listenin' to mean man take on!"

"Tommy," spoke up Grace, "you need to refer to him as Mr.

Mulholland around Trey."

Trey looked at her. "It's all right, Miss Grace. We all know what my father is."

"Preacher man say go bring Little Trey back quick!" Tommy added. "His pappy want him, so I come a-runnin'!"

Trey looked down and breathed sharply. "Wonder what the old devil wants."

"Let's go, Little Trey! He say hurry up!"

"I'll go with you," volunteered Grace.

Trey looked up at her, and then seemed to focus on something beyond. "Here comes Mr. Baker. He can watch after you. I might have to have it out with Father again."

Wash couldn't go on any longer, wondering and fearing and not knowing.

He had pushed ahead, hoping to hear the cry of Sleuth and the second bloodhound on a hot trail. Sleuth may have proven reluctant to pursue the grizzly, but if the dog returned alone and the other hound continued to bay, Wash could at least confirm the quarry. This had gone on too long—nineteen guilt-filled years—and he had to take that rightful shot and end it. The memory of his son demanded no less.

But Joe would never know. He would be just as dead and his grave as forlorn, while Grace still had a lifetime of dreams to fulfill if Wash could undo the great wrong that may have led to the crack of a rifle in the pre-dawn.

Good God, could she have really done it? Could she have followed through on the commitment of a six-year-old and tried to kill Ed Mulholland? How could someone so gentle and caring do such a thing?

Do it, Grace. If I'm never able to, do it for me.

The words came back, powerful words sweeping across the years, the forgotten appeal of a bitter man wrenching a pledge from an innocent child. Again and again, Wash had helped her squeeze a six-shooter's trigger and made her promise, and now the fruits of his deed may have been realized.

That's why he had turned back and pushed hard along the slope, the report of the rifle in the dark haunting him. As the Appaloosa's hoofs sloshed through the melting snow, he rode terrified, expecting to hear at any instant a second shot that would not graze, but kill.

Grace! Don't do it! Don't do it, Grace!

But Grace couldn't hear his silent cry across the distance any better than her six-year-old self could across the years.

When he sighted her ahead, he was relieved, but far from at ease. She held her roan beside a defoliated gray oak, one of many small oaks and pinyons sheltering under columns of algae-covered rock high on the left. Grace had her shoulders to him as she watched Trey and Tommy ride away, and even from here, Wash could hear Tommy's excited voice, although he couldn't make out the words. Just as the two disappeared around a half-dead juniper, Wash drew rein and Grace swung around in the saddle.

"Papa, are you all right?"

She must have seen something in Wash's expression. If his face reflected even a little of what he carried inside, it had to be troubling.

"Grace, I . . . I got to talk to you."

He looked down past his left stirrup as he searched for the right words. The ground was almost clear of snow here, and a sizable log with furrowed bark stretched from the base of the gray oak so that it was parallel to Grace's roan.

"Let's get off a minute," he said.

"All right."

They stepped down as leather complained, and stood in silence as Wash rasped a hand across his bristly face.

"Where's Trey and Tommy off to?" he finally asked.

"Brother Isom sent Tommy to bring him. Mr. Mulholland was carrying on about something."

"Yeah, he carries on about a lot of things."

"Papa . . ."

Wash had been so distracted that only now did he notice the emotion in her voice. For the first time since he had ridden up, he looked squarely at her. Her eyes were moist, and her features curved down as if stripped of the energy that would give them life.

"Darlin', you been cryin'?"

She only hung her head.

"Somethin' to do with Mulholland?" How could anything else be on her mind after trying to kill him?

"Papa, you told me about Joe, how you . . ." She looked up. "Why does Trey think it was his fault?"

"He say that? He was sort of hintin' around but never come out and said it."

"It's got him all torn up. He can't even look at me hardly, 'cause I look so much like Joe."

Wash had never realized it before, but she did have a lot of Joe's features, especially around the eyes.

"What *happened* that night, Papa?" she pressed.

"I think he was fixin' to tell me this mornin' till Mulholland went to hollerin'." He breathed sharply. "*Mulholland.* What he done, gettin' me so wound that night I . . ." He swallowed hard. "Won't ever forgive myself for it, but then I . . . I went and let him eat away at me when you was little."

Wash could almost hear the early morning rifle shot still rolling through the mountains, and he glanced at the .30-30 on Grace's saddle.

Ask her. Ask her straight out.

Twice, he started to but couldn't, and on his third attempt he managed a couple of words before she spoke over him.

"Hold my horse, will you? I'll be right back."

Wash took the reins and watched as she stepped over the log and started up through the scattered pinyons for the privacy she needed to address bodily functions. The stock of the .30-30 rising over the roan's windblown mane seized his attention, and he stared at it, knowing that this was his chance but fearing to act. Securing both horses to a dogleg-shaped branch on the log, he gave a quick look at the concealing brush and forced himself to go around to the off side of Grace's saddle.

The pristine stock jutted up from its boot at an angle, and his hand trembled as he reached for it. He couldn't imagine his palm sweating in this kind of weather, but he could feel the moisture against the oil-stained walnut as he slid the rifle upward. The leather whispered to the friction and suddenly the carbine was out, the smooth, 30-inch barrel brilliant in the sunlight.

Wash wanted to stop. He wanted to slip the rifle back in its boot and pretend that his fears were unfounded, but his grip on the .30-30 grew tighter. He could feel every one of its nine and a half pounds, and more, for it was a burden representing all the years from Grace's young childhood.

With a shudder, he turned the carbine upright and inspected the muzzle. He saw nothing out of the ordinary, just the front sight on edge and the dark circle inside the barrel, but for twenty years he hadn't been able to read without spectacles. The bore was too small to accommodate his little finger, but when he twisted the fleshy pad of his fingertip against the muzzle and withdrew it, his skin briefly showed the imprint and nothing more—or so he chose to believe. In truth, the close-up details were as blurry as words in a book would have been.

But while he may have been unable to see particles as small as gunpowder residue, his olfactory abilities hadn't diminished.

What he didn't know was whether a rifle would still give off an odor after so many hours.

Closing his eyes against his dread, Wash drew the muzzle nearer until the cold steel touched his upper lip.

"What are you doing, Papa?"

He flinched and turned. Grace had descended on the opposite side of the adjacent gray oak and stood staring at him, her face paling and her mouth constricting nervously. For a moment, her wide eyes fell to the carbine.

"Papa," she asked again, "what are you doing?"

Lowering the rifle, Wash saw her as the six-year-old she had been. "What I taught you, way back when, I—"

"Give me the rifle, Papa," interrupted Grace, extending her hand. "Papa, let me have the rifle."

He frowned, not realizing the nature of her concern until he studied her face. "You got it wrong, darlin'."

"I know what this has done to you. The guilt and the hurt. I can't imagine." Her eyes began to well and her voice softened. "Here, let me take the rifle."

He passed it into her care. "I'm not that way. Wouldn't need to use yours, anyhow."

"You sure you're all right?"

"Even with things at their worst, there was your mother to look after. Then you come along."

Still, Grace appeared skeptical.

"I was just lookin' the rifle over," explained Wash. "I guess from where you was, things looked different."

Glancing down, he smoothed the slush with the toe of his boot.

"Grace I . . . I had no right. When you was little, I shouldn't have did what I did."

She squinted in confusion, and Wash went on.

"I heard what you said couple of mornin's ago. About Mulholland. Growin' up and . . . and killin' him.'"

She only looked at Wash, a piercing gaze from which he couldn't turn away.

"You remember, don't you," he said. "All these years later, you remember. My six-shooter and the things I . . . I made you promise."

Her gaze momentarily drifted down to the carbine at her side. "Doesn't he deserve it, Papa?"

How could he answer without a lie showing in his face?

"He's the cause of it all," she continued. "Joe. What it's done to you. Even Trey not wanting to be around me, I guess. Ed Mulholland's the cause of it all."

She was right.

Damn it, she was right.

"Never should've made it your responsibility," he said. "You was just six. I had no call."

"Is that what I was? Six?"

"Anyhow, I imagine the Good Lord's got His own way of dealin' with Mulholland."

Wash was surprised—confounded was more like it—to hear such words come out of his mouth. Just hours before, he had relived in dream his baptism, and now this. What was the matter with him?

When Grace looked again at the .30-30, Wash focused on the muzzle. Caught unawares as she had come up behind him, he hadn't checked for an odor to his satisfaction.

"Grace, this mornin' before daylight. I've got to know."

She only set her blue eyes on him, and then he turned with her toward sudden gunshots, quick reports echoing over one another.

"Back where Trey and Tommy went," she said.

"Three in a row. Somebody signalin' maybe."

Mounting up, Wash took his Appaloosa back along the

Patrick Dearen

mountainside at the hindquarter of Grace's roan. Again and again, he saw her look over her shoulder at him, worry lines in her face. Wash hadn't gotten the denial he so desperately needed, and it was clear that she was as uneasy about his state of mind as he was about hers.

174

CHAPTER SEVENTEEN

"You speak Mex better than me, Baker. See where in the hell she come from."

Wash and Grace had dropped back down to a valley and the edge of a sprawling meadow, the surrounding evergreens in sharp distinction to its wavy blue grama. Grazing in the sun were twenty-five or thirty Herefords, among several bunches of free-ranging cattle Wash had come upon during the hunt. Beside the thick pinyons under the rising slope on the left, Mulholland was sitting on a log and pointing. At first, Wash couldn't see through all the horses and dismounted riders, but as he advanced, he was stunned to find a Mexican girl, no more than nine. She looked up, and he had never seen a face so ashen or the tissue underneath anyone's eyes so puffy and red.

But Mulholland was preoccupied with Trey, whose features clearly showed impatience as he stood before the rancher.

"I'm a-sufferin', son," said Mulholland. "Been shot and chewed on and ever'thing else. You got to look after me, old as I'm gettin'." He slung an arm toward the grazing cattle. "Down in the grass yonder's a half-eat carcass with our brand on it. Damned grizzly! Reminded me how we's got to work together. Not just to hunt that thing down, but in our cow business. You got to take over 'fore long. That's why I sent for you. Let ever'body ride on so's we can talk by ourselves."

Trey, however, wasn't interested, and as Wash drew rein, the young man turned.

"Mr. Baker, the girl came down off the mountain soon as Tommy and I rode up. None of us speak Spanish very well, so I'm glad you came when I fired the shots."

Tension showed in the girl's uplifted eyebrows and in the way her lower lip pushed up. Glistening beads rolled down between her drooping nose and pronounced cheekbones, and more emotion welled in her dark eyes. A red-and-gray-banded serape, brushed by raven hair, wrapped her shoulders, but even from a few yards away, Wash could see her tremble.

"What are you doin' here by yourself?" asked Wash in Spanish. Maybe it was a man's way, seeking a direct answer instead of first attending to a person's pressing needs.

But Grace, whose Spanish was as good as Wash's, spoke up before the girl could reply. "You're cold, aren't you, *chiquita*? Here, put my coat on."

Stepping down, Grace passed the reins to Trey and removed her coat. Wash watched with both shame and pride as she approached the girl and draped the woolen garment over her small shoulders; he supposed he could learn a few things from his daughter about sensitivity.

"I imagine she's hungry too," Wash said as he dismounted. Hitching the Appaloosa to a low-hanging limb, he addressed Tommy, who looked on wide-eyed. "Get her some water, would you, Tommy?"

"I sure do it, Mr. Wash. Poor thing looks plum' wore down."

Searching the saddlebag behind the cantle, Wash withdrew airtights and a spoon and gained the muchacha's attention.

"Frijoles? Tomates?" he asked.

When the girl nodded, he set the cans on a knee-high boulder at the Appaloosa's hindquarter and punctured the tops with his pocketknife. Cutting an *X* from rim to rim in each, he peeled the jags back and placed the spoon inside the beans. Meanwhile, away from the grumbling Mulholland, Grace had sat the girl on a log, and the muchacha sipped from a canteen as Wash walked up.

"Careful and don't cut yourself," he warned, setting the airtights beside her. "*Frijoles* is cold, but they'll still be good."

At first, the girl's sobs kept her from eating much, but after she forced down a few bites her appetite improved. As Wash waited patiently, he noticed that Grace stood with arms crossed, clearly for purposes of warmth.

"Here, darlin'," he said, taking off his coat.

"I'm all right, Papa."

Spreading the garment from the back, Wash held it up and let her slip it on. "You was thinkin' and I wasn't. One more way I hadn't set a good example."

Soon the muchacha had eaten her fill. Already, her color seemed to have improved, but her eyes stayed as sad as ever.

Wash continued to hover over the girl. "I'm Mr. Wash. That's my daughter Grace there. *Cómo te llamas?*"

It had never occurred to him that his position might seem intimidating, but the girl wouldn't make eye contact and replied only in a meek whisper.

"Benita."

"Oh what a pretty name!" spoke up Grace, drawing the girl's attention. "It comes from Latin for *blessed*. Did you know that?"

Benita shook her head, but Grace's friendly way seemed to open a door. When Grace eased down on her right, Benita turned to her.

"Benita," repeated Grace, with a finger under her own lip. "If I ever have a little girl, I can't think of a better name!"

Was that the hint of a bittersweet smile on Benita's face?

Grace looked up at Wash, as if deferring the questioning to him.

"You go ahead, darlin'," he told her in English. "You's doin' better with her."

"Where's your family, Benita?" Grace asked.

The girl's voice choked. "I don't have anybody."

"No one?"

Distress wrenched Benita's face, and Grace slipped an arm about her. The touch released the floodgates of the girl's emotions, and she fell into Grace's embrace and wept until her small frame seemed unable to quake any more. Wash knew as well as anyone what grief was, and as his daughter looked up over the child's head nestled in her nape, it was all he could do to maintain his composure.

But as Wash witnessed Grace's kindness and compassion, something else troubled him more. If he was to blame for leading someone so virtuous into turning a rifle against another— even if his name was Ed Mulholland—what did that say about Wash's chances for forgiveness?

Emma . . . Emma . . .

I want to believe again.

"How did you come to be out here, Benita?" Grace asked as she stroked the girl's hair.

"Rosindo . . . Rosindo," she sobbed. "He never came back! I told him I wouldn't have anybody. I told my brother if he died like Papá I wouldn't have anybody!"

It took several minutes and gentle coaxing by Grace, but eventually Wash pieced together an incredible story of a girl and her twelve-year-old brother tracking *el oso plateado*, the silver bear, all the way from their father's mauled body in the Fronterizas in Mexico. When the trail had gone cold, they had been guided by a man in black whom they believed to be their father's restless spirit. Most striking, her brother had been driven by the conviction that the only way to free their father's soul was if he killed the great bear before the next full moon rose an hour in the sky.

When Wash turned and related the gist of the muchacha's

story, Mulholland had no reaction, choosing instead to continue grumbling. Isom, too, looked on without comment, but Trey proved once again that he was more than his father's son.

"What are we to make of this, Mr. Baker?" he asked.

"Poor girl's not makin' it up, takin' on like she is."

"We need to go look for her brother. If she didn't find any sign of him, he could still be out there, thinking she's dead like she thinks he is."

"Yeah, and wonderin' what to do. Whether to spend the rest of the day lookin' for her, or stay after the grizzly."

Trey looked confused.

"My Mexican hands are awful superstitious," Wash explained. "If they believe somethin', they'll hang with it to the end. If that brother of hers come all this way 'cause of what some healer said, I expect he'll try to finish what he started, providin' he's still alive. You know what comes tonight, don't you?"

Trey's silence persisted.

"Full moon," Wash went on. "Turns out, we's after the same thing, only he's got to get it done quick." Then he turned to Grace. "Tell her she needs to take us to the last place she saw him. But don't say nothin' to get her hopes up."

"Mr. Baker, knowing what we do about the girl's brother clears up a mystery."

With Benita guiding as she rode double behind Grace, Wash and the other riders ascended eastward through dense timber to the creak of saddles and the grate of slipping hoofs in patches of snow. The beaten game trail promised to carry them up between a lofty rock rim, rising and falling through the pinyons on the left, and another mountain across from it. Although less rugged, the latter summit tossed through the limbs with the same flowing rhythm, as the Appaloosa nodded along and kept pace behind Trey's dun.

"I guess it solves not just one mystery," continued Trey, looking back at Wash, "but maybe two."

"How you figure?" Wash asked.

"That gunshot in the canyon that kept the bear from mauling you. Couldn't have been anyone else."

"Yeah, must've been." Wash pondered things a moment. "What's the second?"

"What happened in the dark of the morning, Father getting shot. Must've been a stray bullet from their camp."

Through the interlaced limbs beyond Trey, Wash studied the back of Grace's shoulders above the muchacha's dark hair.

"Yeah," Wash said doubtfully. "Providin' it was a accident."

Trey twisted around in the saddle and faced him. "Mr. Baker, you think the boy shot in our camp on purpose?"

Do it, Grace. If I'm never able to, do it for me.

In an instant, Wash was back in the past, kneeling again with a little girl as he helped her apply the five pounds of pressure necessary to pull the trigger of his revolver. With the recoil of every discharge, she stumbled back against him, and as the gunshot resounded, so did his demand that this blameless child commit to an unspeakable vow.

He's there, Grace, down the sights. Kill him for me. If I can't ever do it, kill Ed Mulholland for me.

In her little girl's voice, Grace had given her word, and now she had tried to follow through.

"Mr. Baker?" Trey asked again.

But Wash had nothing to say, and they rode on in silence for a while, so many things beleaguering him. Grace's long-ago pledge, he couldn't discuss with anyone, and with Isom and his bay within earshot behind, Wash couldn't bring up the Concho and whatever Trey had yet to reveal about that night. No matter its nature, it had impacted Trey's relationship with Grace, and she didn't need anything else standing in the way of the bright future she deserved.

Trey's thoughts, too, obviously turned to Grace, who had managed to engage the grieving muchacha to the point that Wash could hear them talking constantly.

"Miss Grace, she . . . she's wonderful," said Trey, looking toward her admiringly. "She takes such an interest in everyone. That poor little girl's lost so much, and look how she's already taken to Miss Grace."

"Yeah," acknowledged Wash. "She's got a gift that way."

"I . . . I never meant to trifle with her feelings."

Wash reflexively straightened in his daughter's defense. "That what you done? I found her cryin' earlier."

From behind Trey's dun, Wash saw the young man shrug. "I told you she deserves better than me."

"None of my affair, but whatever come between y'all, I wish you'd make it right."

Trey looked back. "It can't be undone, Mr. Baker. My Lord, I'd give anything—*anything.*"

"Somethin' to do with what you started tellin' me?" From what Grace had said, Wash already knew the answer. "We need to get off by ourselves someplace and talk."

"It's a talk I need to finish with Miss Grace too." Trey's voice grew hoarse with emotion. "Maybe she could . . . she could put me behind her then."

"That what you want? Don't think she does, unhappy as she is. Never thought I'd regret things not workin' out between her and a Mulholland."

Wash hadn't meant to say *Mulholland,* especially with the contempt he always applied to it, but he wasn't going to apologize. For a moment though, as the roan in the lead angled up through the brush, he focused on his daughter, who hadn't even been born yet during that drive in '80.

"Guess a lot of things we's dealin' with goes back to the

Concho," said Wash, dwelling on the dark cloud that threatened her future. "What went on that night won't let none of us alone."

With every pace of the roan down the far side of the forested pass, it was as if an imp perched on Grace's shoulder and whispered in her ear.

Do it.

Kill him.

Kill Ed Mulholland.

She had never felt so powerful a summons, one that had lain dormant since childhood and now rose up, trying to wrest control of the young woman she had become.

He caused it all.

Joe.

Papa.

Trey.

Kill Ed Mulholland.

She heard the call with the ears of both a child and a woman, and with it came the repeated roar of a six-shooter unwieldy in small hands.

Do it.

Kill him.

Kill Ed Mulholland.

Grace wished that Benita, clinging from behind, hadn't gone silent, so that the girl's voice might compete with the relentless charge. But as soon as the roan had reached the top of the pass, between a sunlit cliff on the left and a pinyon-studded slope on the right, Benita's head had fallen against Grace's shoulder. Exhausted physically and emotionally, the muchacha had lapsed into merciful sleep, while the summons was more alive than ever, tormenting and prodding Grace toward an unforgivable act.

But she was also worried about her father's frame of mind,

and she looked back through a latticework of pinyon needles to reassure herself. Past the dun and Trey's uncharacteristically stooped shoulders, Wash seemed all right astride the Appaloosa, but the sight of him raised disturbing memories of his whispers.

There'll be a time and place, Grace. Maybe you'll be all growed up. Maybe I won't be here no more to help. But a time and place is comin'.

All these years later, she could still picture the flush in her father's face and the swollen veins at his temples.

We got to kill him, Grace. We got to kill Ed Mulholland in a way so's nobody will know.

And the call to action was too powerful for Grace to ignore.

"The poor darlin's all in, looks like."

Until her father's quiet remark, Grace was so vexed by the memories that she didn't realize that the roan had leveled out in a canyon's wooded depths. She looked to her left, finding him abreast on the Appaloosa but still seeing him for a brief moment as he had been in her childhood. He must have read the blank look in her eyes, for he nodded to Benita.

"The girl," he said. "Don't know how she'll ever deal with this."

Grace glanced over her shoulder at the *muchacha*, who had begun to stir. "She's so lost, Papa," responded Grace in English. "She keeps telling me everyone's dead and she doesn't have a home anywhere."

Her father winced. "Tell the poor darlin' not to fret. If it comes to it, we got a place for her."

"I already told her. I knew you and Mama would take her in, same as you did Tommy."

"He was a half-growed boy, workin' for me. Course, he wasn't ever goin' to grow up. A youngster eight or nine might be bitin' off more we can chew, old as we are, but I know your mother wouldn't turn her out in the cold any more than I would."

Compassion. It was one of her father's traits that Grace admired most, and she couldn't reconcile it with how he felt about Ed Mulholland. Still, in light of the frightful vow that had all but seized control of her, she could have said the same about herself.

All the way from the meadow to this tangled bank before a rock-bottom drainage, Mulholland had blown his police whistle to recall his remaining hound. Now as Grace reined up at Benita's instruction between a buckeye and hackberry across from a dark fissure, the black-and-tan dog came running up from down-canyon. Following in the hound's wake was Sleuth, hobbling but slinging foam in his enthusiasm to greet Tommy, who had stepped off his horse.

"There's good ol' dog!" Tommy exclaimed, stooping to pet the animal.

Meanwhile, Wash brought his Appaloosa alongside Grace's roan. "This the place?" he asked Benita in Spanish.

"Sí."

"Go ahead and climb off and we'll go over there."

Grace felt Benita's cheek press against her back as if the girl tried to hide.

"What's the matter?" Wash gently asked the muchacha. "Come show us."

The delicate arms tightened around Grace's midriff. "I don't want to go! I don't want to go!"

Grace reached around and patted Benita on the shoulder. "It's all right, Benita. Nothing can get you now. I'll go with you."

"No! No! No!"

It was a word that meant the same in English as in Spanish, but even if no one had understood, there could be no mistaking Benita's body language.

"Nobody's goin' to make you do somethin' you don't want to," Wash told her. "You just go ahead and stay here with Grace."

He dismounted and hitched the Appaloosa, but not until he started down for the fissure with his shotgun did the muchacha relax her grip.

"Let's climb off and stretch our legs, Benita," Grace suggested.

The ground was soft but not muddy as they stepped down, and the grama grass rustled against Grace's boot uppers as she led the roan to the adjacent hackberry and tied it. Trey and Isom had accompanied Wash, and so had Tommy and Sleuth. The dog stopped to lap water from a pool, but the men continued on to the draping fern that partially concealed the opening. When her father probed behind the greenery with the shotgun barrel, Grace turned away and found Benita watching, her eyes wide in anxiety.

Grace couldn't imagine the girl's fear and grief.

"Benita, I've got something for you."

Grace stepped around her and drew the muchacha's attention away from the fissure. Rummaging in a saddlebag, she produced a hair brush and extended it.

"You have such pretty hair," said Grace. "I'll bet it's like silk when it's brushed out!"

With Benita occupied with grooming, Grace glanced across the drainage and saw Trey edge inside the fissure. With his avowal of love, she yearned for him more than ever, aching to a kind of pain she hadn't realized existed, and yet a gulf as wide as this canyon separated them.

And all because of the tragedy provoked by Ed Mulholland.

Mulholland was down off his sorrel and taking a nip from a flask, the red spider veins of a drunkard showing in his cheeks, nose, and V of his neck. Abruptly, Grace saw him as she had in imagination as a child: down the sights of a glinting six-gun.

Thirteen years had passed since that moment, and here the filthy devil was, still bringing evil on everything he touched.

Do it, Grace.

Kill Ed Mulholland.

"You don't care, do you." For an instant Grace wasn't aware that her thoughts had become spoken words.

Mulholland looked up, his eyebrows pinching.

"What you've done," continued Grace, "all you've caused, you don't care."

"You got somethin' in your craw, girl?" he asked.

"Joe. Papa. Trey. Me. You ruin lives and you don't care."

He toyed with his earlobe. "What in hell you talkin' about?"

"You go on like nothing happened. But the people you've wronged still pay the price."

Mulholland rubbed the back of his neck. "I-god, you Bakers are somethin'. Warned that boy of mine to stay away from your kind."

Grace hadn't known that, but she could still see Mulholland viciously lash Trey with a quirt, and Trey in turn tear the whip from his grasp. Just as telling had been the way that Trey had responded with cold indifference to his father's subsequent pleas for attention.

"I guess you pay a price too," she said. "Your own son knows what you are and won't forget it."

Grace turned away, the summons to kill stronger than ever.

CHAPTER EIGHTEEN

"Crying . . . always crying. I was by the fireplace and the child kept crying. I was by the fire but it was like I was in it."

Isom, rocking to his bay's gait just ahead of Wash, had muttered to himself ever since the party had started southward up the canyon on horseback.

"Yes, in hellfire," Isom went on. "Looking out from hellfire . . . watching the shadows . . . Yes, the shadows dancing . . . dancing shadows . . . Imps out of perdition."

Wash and the others had found no indication that Rosindo had ever returned to the fissure, and only echoes had responded to their shouts in a three-mile ride down the gulch. Turning back, they had ridden past the fissure and continued on, but thus far the search up-canyon had proven just as fruitless.

With what Benita had related—her brother venturing from the crevice to fight *el oso plateado*—Wash no longer had any hope for the boy. The grizzly's power, Wash had seen for himself, and as much as he admired the muchacho's courage, a mere child with a knife would have stood no chance.

Maybe the righteous shotgun blast so craved by Wash could also avenge.

Just minutes ago, the zigzagging hounds had picked up a hot trail and raced ahead in full cry. Above Isom's mumble, Wash could distinguish Sleuth's croak even at a distance, and so could Tommy from behind Wash's Appaloosa, for the red-haired man shouted encouragement.

"Get him, ol' dog! Trail Mr. Grizzly out!"

But Wash wasn't so sure of the hounds' quarry; even the female had chased after a mountain lion and a black bear.

"The child . . . the child," continued Isom, dodging a pinyon limb. "Crying louder and louder and . . ."

The preacher brushed another limb and left it spring-loaded so that it slapped the Appaloosa's forehead, causing the horse to shy.

"Warn me next time, would you?" spoke up Wash. "Limb caught my horse in the face."

But Isom, lost in his own world, only persisted in his murmurs.

"Crying and crying . . . Make him stop . . . Please make him stop . . ."

Over the last few days, Wash had grown accustomed to hearing Isom talk to himself, but never had his voice seemed this pained. It was almost a sob, and Wash felt for him, knowing all that had been taken from the preacher in the span of two weeks. After the Concho tragedy, Wash would have lost his reason without Emma, and yet Isom carried his burden alone.

"You all right, Brother Isom?" Wash asked.

The clergyman reined up, and his black cutaway coat flared as he turned the bay to Wash. For all the disquiet in Isom's voice, it was nothing compared to the distress behind the steel-wire spectacles.

"He . . . he *killed* her, Brother Baker," Isom whispered. "Just being born, he *killed* my Lela."

"You got to quit thinkin' like that," said Wash. "Just makes things worse. Grab yourself by the bootstraps and pull yourself out of it."

"It's more than a man can do, Brother Baker. It's more than *I* can do."

"Then get the Good Lord . . ." There it was again, a reminder of the faith Wash once had lived by, unexpectedly showing itself.

"The Lord . . . Yes, the Lord." Now, Isom seemed to speak to himself again. "Our sins . . . Terrible sins . . . He is faithful and just to forgive. Confess . . . Just confess . . ."

As they rode on, skirting ash and maple interspersed with occasional ponderosas, Sleuth's hoarse bark from ahead seemed to lose its vigor. He began to cry only intermittently and finally went quiet, while the other hound continued to bay as spirited as ever. Several minutes later, as the Appaloosa entered a sunny meadow, Wash wasn't surprised to find Sleuth waiting in the well-grazed grama.

"There's good ol' dog!" exclaimed Tommy.

But Sleuth seemed to realize that Wash was his master, for he studied Wash penitently and gave a half-hearted wag of his tail. When Wash drew rein, the dog slunk toward him with head lowered submissively, the tail persisting in its tentative wag. Clearly, the hound expected a thrashing.

"I'm not Mulholland," said Wash, not caring who might hear. "You's not in any trouble."

But Sleuth wasn't reassured, for the dog sank and placed his jaw flush on the ground, his floppy ears splayed to the sides. It was almost heartbreaking how the hazel eyes looked up at Wash so forlornly.

Wash knew what Joe would have done. The yellow hound that had mourned at his grave—Wash knew what Joe would have done.

Stepping off the Appaloosa, Wash knelt in the grama and smoothed his hand across the baggy skin that crinkled Sleuth's head.

"Sure a good dog, ain't he, Mr. Wash?"

Until he heard the voice, Wash wasn't aware that Tommy had dismounted and come up at his shoulder.

"One with smarts, too, Tommy." Sleuth had begun licking

Wash's fingers. "He's tellin' me this isn't a black bear or lion they's trailin'."

"Sure 'nough?"

Wash's fingers were wet with slobber as he gazed down the hound's wrinkled backbone to the woods beyond the meadow.

"Yeah, he knows, don't you, ol' boy." He looked back into the dog's eyes. "You's smart enough not to tangle with a grizzly bear."

Isom also had drawn rein, and from the stirrups of the bay, he resumed his quiet monologue.

"The bear . . . Yes, the bear . . . Jehovah's agent of judgment . . . a bear lying in wait . . . ready to tear asunder."

Wash felt a hand clutch his shoulder.

"Mr. Wash? Mr. Wash?"

Wash turned to find a paling Tommy cast wide eyes toward the clergyman.

"What's got you spooked, Tommy?" asked Wash.

"Preacher man. He say we ain't huntin' Mr. Grizzly. Mr. Grizzly huntin' *us.*"

Wash looked around at Isom, whose lips now moved silently. Wash hadn't heard Isom make such a statement outright, but there was something eerie about the notion in light of the clergyman's story of judgment meted out by bears against the mockers of Elisha.

As their horses climbed steadily through a natural arbor of tall ponderosas that yielded sunlight only grudgingly, Wash could hear Mulholland weeping.

At first, Wash hadn't been certain, and his position behind the rancher's sorrel didn't allow a direct look at his features. For several minutes, the clues had been there: the hunched figure, the hanging Stetson, the elbow braced against ribs as if shielding the eyes from the world. Most telling, his shoulder blades moved in a way that couldn't be explained by the sorrel's nodding gait up through small boulders green-tinged with lichen. Now, however, Mulholland's quiet sobs confirmed it.

Where the snow had melted, Wash and the others had dismounted and led their tiring horses a mile or more, but the slush in this stand of ponderosas had forced them back into the stirrups. Sometimes the pines ahead broke just enough for Wash to glimpse sunlit palisades rearing above green-timbered slopes, and above the cliffs, a mountain's wooded shoulders. Capping all was a fist of rock, carved out of the blue of the sky.

As daunting as Sawtooth had been, it paled before this peak known as Baldy or Livermore, a summit, still miles away, of more than eight thousand feet, or so a surveyor had said. Mulholland, for all his bluster, may have been right about a grizzly seeking rocky heights, for the cry of the black-and-tan hound seemed to come from a direct line to Baldy's uppermost reaches. Even Sleuth, emboldened now that he was back with the party, occasionally bayed as he trotted down the trail ahead of the horses. Nevertheless, the dog got no farther than a stone's throw beyond Grace, whose roan led the way a length in front of Mulholland's sorrel.

Wash liked her there, in plain sight every moment, her blonde tresses playing against her back in contrast to the dark hair of her young ward. He didn't have to worry what Grace might be doing, for she was a portrait of innocence so unlike the image he had of the person behind the rifle shot in the dark.

Mulholland continued to weep, loudly enough for Grace to look back. She surveyed the rancher only briefly, and then made eye contact with Wash. As her gaze lingered, it seemed to convey everything she had promised him as a child—closing her hand on a firearm grip, sliding her finger inside a trigger guard, lining up a swaying front sight so that it locked on a man who deserved to die.

Don't do it, Grace.

Please don't ever go and do it.

"Baker." Mulholland had turned in the saddle.

"Yeah?" asked Wash.

Mulholland motioned with his head and slowed his sorrel, allowing Wash to approach on the left. Mulholland was the last person with whom Wash wanted to ride, but as soon as the Appaloosa caught up, the rancher urged the sorrel onward so that the horses stayed abreast.

With Mulholland's emotions on display, Wash felt uneasy—embarrassed was more like it—so he paid the man only a glance. For a while, they rode in silence, Mulholland's chin against his chest. Even when the rancher spoke, Wash continued to focus on the distorted tracks in the slush ahead.

"How . . ." Between the liquor on his breath and his emotions, Mulholland had difficulty voicing words. "How was it you was always so close to your boy?"

"Never figured you noticed."

"I . . . I'd give anything to have it like you did. Tell me what you done different."

Wash breathed sharply. "Never took a ridin' whip to him, for one thing."

For several paces of their horses, that shut Mulholland up, but eventually he managed more quiet words.

"I-god, I . . . I got nothin'. My own boy . . . lost him . . . My own . . . I-god, nothin', and you and . . ."

A hell of place he's come to if he's lookin' for sympathy.

Mulholland's voice choked more. "Ever' damned mile, I hated it. Seein' you and your boy get along . . . I hated ever' mile of that drive."

"Least, you still had yours when it was done with."

For long seconds, there were only muffled hoofbeats to compete with the bad memories.

"I should've gone to the buryin', Baker."

I didn't want you there, you bastard.

The rancher went on. "Should've been there, but I . . . I couldn't bring myself to, knowin' I . . ."

Wash turned to Mulholland, and Mulholland turned to him, two men overwhelmed by a tragedy that had shaped so many lives.

"My doin'," said Mulholland. "You shootin' your boy—my doin', same as yours."

Wash could only puzzle over his words and listen.

"Got ever'body on edge, just 'cause I could. Never meant for . . ." Mulholland brought a hand to his eyes and began to weep again. "Guess your girl's right—I . . . I got nothin'. Even my own boy knows what I am."

When Wash looked out over his Appaloosa's ears, he found Grace twisted around on the roan and staring.

Chapter Nineteen

Leading the lame roan, Rosindo struggled up a forested slope through a dark cloud that choked the life from him.

Mamá . . . Papá . . . Benita—one and all, they had cruelly been taken away. Now, in the lonely midnight of his fear, the boy had no reason to take another step except for the impossible hope of a reunion beyond the dying sun.

Soon, day would end and a full moon would appear on the horizon hidden by the imposing peak on Rosindo's left. As the uncaring orb rose into the sky, it would reach the critical moment quickly, and if *el oso plateado* still lived, Rosindo would lose everything.

Everything!

It was too much for a mere boy to shoulder, but ahead, always ahead, the faceless shadow of his father lured him higher into this stronghold where immense mountains crowded him.

Earlier, Rosindo had felt the splash of water as the roan had forded a trickling stream. With the canyon lands behind, the hoofs had carried him up an undulating course through white-leaf oaks and wild cherries, and underneath red-barked ponderosas and seventy-foot limber pines. Across his path, rocky ravines had swept down from the heights, the clawing briars in their tangled depths bloodying the roan's breast. But not until the horse had dipped its nose had Rosindo dismounted and found the animal tipping a front hoof on edge to avoid bearing weight.

Now, all Rosindo could do was sob the names of everyone he had loved and trudge on with reins in hand through the numbing slush.

He broke out on a high, narrow saddle between a three-hundred-foot wooded prominence on his left and a much steeper rise on the right. Light-headed, he bent over with his hands on his knees and labored for breath. He thought his chest would never stop heaving, but when he looked out over the scene before him, his physical travails were forgotten.

Between tall, straight ponderosas, swaying in a moaning wind, lesser mountains unfurled into the distance like wrinkles on the old *curandero*'s face. But there was more, a startling sight where the land flattened against the horizon: a full moon emerging.

One hour.

That's all Rosindo had.

One hour.

He felt strangely compelled to turn and look up alongside the ridge on his right. Its contours hid much, and so did the ponderosas and whiteleaf oaks, but a thousand or so feet higher, and perhaps a mile west-southwest, he could make out a summit fist of rock shining coppery in the rays of the setting sun.

And standing not twenty paces away from him and beckoning to its heights was his father's *bulto*.

"Dare you . . . Dare you . . . Dare you . . ."

All the way up from a canyon head, a five-hundred-foot pitch too steep for a horse to carry a heavy rider, Trey had found breath enough to talk to himself. Now, as he paused alongside his dun just above Grace, she saw him suspended in the sky, for there was no higher mountain beyond him.

For Grace, leading her roan while Benita rode, it had been a grueling ascent between stony outcrops. The miles since Rockpile had worn on Grace, but the emotional toll had been worse.

She grappled with issues that no nineteen-year-old girl should, and they were more than she could bear. So many things hinged on what had happened on a night before she had been born, and yet love wasn't enough for the person who had been at Joe's side to tell her.

"Dare you . . . Dare you . . . Dare you . . ."

It was all that Trey had said during the climb, and he still muttered the words as Grace broke breathless onto a ridge. Bare except for remnants of the big snow, it fell away dramatically only yards ahead. With a wind in her face that only eagles knew, she could see far into Mexico to the south and felt as if she were on top of the world. Still, a crag rose three hundred feet immediately on her right, while two hundred yards in the opposite direction, back to the east where the hound bayed, eminences soared one atop another to a summit fist of rock that her father called Baldy.

"Dare you . . . Dare you . . ."

"What are you saying, Trey?"

He stood with head down, his stooped profile and that of the dun's angular face framing Baldy's sun-splashed cliffs.

"You need to move on from me," he said without looking up. "In your life, you need to move on, Miss Grace."

With Benita not understanding English, Grace felt that she and Trey had a measure of privacy.

"You're not doing me fair," she said with emotion. "You can't tell me you love me and do this without telling me why."

Trey glanced at Benita and secured his dun to a small boulder. When he started away along the ridge, Grace passed Benita the reins of her horse and followed.

"Please, Trey. Please tell me."

The young man stopped, keeping the back of his slumping shoulders to her. "There's no other way, I guess. Getting you to move on, I guess there's no other way."

He straightened to a deep breath and turned. Tension built around his eyes, and just as he began to speak, something averted his gaze.

"Here comes Mr. Baker. I just want to tell this once."

Grace checked and found her father topping out with his Appaloosa.

"Papa?" she called.

Wash seemed all but spent as he faced her, but he wrapped the reins of his horse around a jutting rock and approached. He must have anticipated the nature of their parley, for he came up alongside Grace with a question for Trey.

"This the time?"

"Yes, sir. For Miss Grace's sake. So . . . So she can put me behind her."

He told a story of two best friends on the adventure of their lives, mere boys daring one another to see who would back down first. Wild broncs and bedroll salamanders and violations of chuck wagon etiquette—nothing had been off limits. And then had come a storm-tossed night when Wash had warned everyone in camp not to venture into the pitch-black where a man-killer prowled.

"You told us, Mr. Baker," recounted Trey. " 'Don't go off unless you just have to. If somebody sees something, challenge it before you shoot. And for God's sake, if you're the one challenged, answer quick and loud.' You told us, Mr. Baker, you told Joe and me both when we crawled in our bedroll, but I wouldn't let Joe go to sleep."

Trey winced and shuddered visibly before continuing.

" 'Why don't you run way out past the wagon,' I told him. 'See if you can stay out there till it thunders three times.'

" 'Not me,' he says. 'Ain't budging a step from the fire.'

" 'Scaredy-cat. Bet you're white as a wagon sheet.'

" 'You heard what Papa said. If the bear don't get me,

somebody's liable to shoot.'

" 'Dare you, Joe!'

"Told you, I ain't doing it.'

" 'Dare you! Dare you!'

" 'Quit it, Trey. You'd get me killed.'

" 'Dare you! Dare you! Dare you!' "

Grace saw Trey's blue eyes begin to well, and he had to pause before he could go on.

"I kept after him, shaming him, not giving a thought to what could happen. 'All right, all right,' I finally get him to say. 'But you got to come too.'

"We circle behind the wagon and can't see a thing besides lightning, but we could imagine plenty. I don't know if it was me or Joe that said something first, but we started running back. I see a shape between us and the fire, and somebody asks who we are, and I'm yelling our names and I guess Joe is too. But the thunder's so loud I can't hear my own voice, and the next thing I know, a shotgun goes off and the best friend I ever had is dead—because of me."

His cheeks glistening and lower lip quaking, Trey was the height of despondency as his head dropped to the V of his collar.

"Now you know," he said. "You *both* know. The wrong boy died that night."

Grieving for Trey's misspent years of regret, Grace went closer. But her father was already there, placing a hand on the young man's shoulder, and she couldn't have been more surprised.

"Nobody blamin' you, son," said Wash, unable to contain his emotions. "You was just a boy. Nobody blamin' you. Some things was just meant to be."

Grace was no less moved. "Papa's right," she whispered, drawing Trey's eyes. "Nothing's changed. You and me, nothing's changed. I love you just as much—*more.*"

When Trey opened his arm, she went into his embrace, and on a mountaintop far removed from the Concho tragedy, the three of them wept for a boy dead nineteen years. Yet in a moment filled with hope, a voice more powerful than ever pushed Grace closer to an inevitable hour.

Kill him.

Kill Ed Mulholland.

CHAPTER TWENTY

Some things was just meant to be.

Wash had said it, but it better befitted someone of faith. As the Appaloosa carried him higher, dodging great folds of burnished rock and tracing the brink of a five-hundred-foot drop, he wondered again what was taking place in the part of him that once had lived every day secure in the will of a Higher Power. The rustle as his horse broke through thickets of scrub oak and small, slender aspens, none taller than his head, was like the rush of the Spirit-filled wind about which Isom had preached, and he seemed to see in the loftiest peaks the foundations of Heaven toward which he was being borne on eagles' wings.

Emma . . . Emma . . .

I want to believe again.

"Don't hear him no more, Mr. Wash."

Wash looked back, half-blinded by the low-hanging sun. He found Tommy on the dapple gray just behind and the other riders strung out along a hogback.

"That ol' hound dog," added Tommy. "Mean man's dog."

Wash straightened in the saddle and listened as he studied the way ahead. Indeed, there was nothing now but the howl of the wind.

"Out of range, I guess," he said.

Or dead, he started to add, but there was no reason to upset Tommy unnecessarily.

"Ol' sun sure a-fallin', ain't it."

"Yeah, got to find us a place to make dry camp, Tommy. Not much time to do it in."

"I be along quick. Got to step off and tighten this ol' cinch."

Up through a deep, narrow passage between sheer rock, Wash pushed on, led by Sleuth. But the dog grew apprehensive and soon fell back to within yards of the Appaloosa. Just as the horse started left around a huge dome sparkling with ice, Sleuth turned and retreated, his tail tucked between his legs as he looked back fearfully. When Wash reined up, watching the hound slink past the Appaloosa, Isom rode by, followed by Mulholland, who slouched in the saddle more than ever.

"Don't like the looks of this," said Wash, reaching for his shotgun. "Brother Isom, Mulholland, that bear must be up there."

Isom pulled away on the bay without comment, but Mulholland held his sorrel and gave a sigh of resignation. He was like a dead man riding, pale and lifeless, but he had the awareness to slide his .30-40 out of its saddle boot.

"Don't know how come I'm still out here," he said in his dead man's voice. "Got nothin' . . . nothin' . . . My own boy . . . Bear might as well eat ever' cow I got. It all ends with me anyhow."

When Mulholland rode on, Wash fell in behind, and soon the Appaloosa negotiated a natural staircase and broke onto a bare flat forty yards across. Ahead and to the right, a half mile maybe, Baldy rose another four hundred feet, its rocky fist taking on a reddish hue in the setting sun. On the left of the flat were dormant elderberry trees, their arching, woody stems forming a dense wall eight feet high with sage and green catchweed bedstraw at the base. At eleven o'clock, the elderberries ended at rimrock that resembled a sawblade laid flat, with its teeth jutting out over a precipice. Far below, Wash could see the upper reaches of a rugged colonnade, fading in the dying light, while deep shadows already covered the forested canyons in the distance.

He took a closer look at the flat with its patchy snow. The grizzly couldn't be far ahead, but nightfall was imminent.

"Better make camp here," he said to no one in particular. "I'm ridin' on a ways."

"Papa?"

Wash reined his horse about. Grace was nearing on her roan, followed at a considerable distance by Trey and Tommy.

"What is it, darlin'?" asked Wash as she halted.

"Wait for first light, Papa. You could ride off a cliff. Wait for first light."

"Bear's got to be close, way Sleuth's actin'. Look at the poor thing, way back behind Tommy. If I don't get a shot quick, I'll be back and get my horse staked out."

Grace persisted in her appeal as she helped Benita dismount and did so herself. Wash was anxious to press on, but he listened patiently before checking the flat. Isom was on foot in the slush and wandering aimlessly toward the elderberry trees, while Mulholland had drawn rein near the rimrock and still sat his horse like a man more dead than alive.

For me, Grace. Kill him for me.

Wash didn't like the abrupt memory, and he turned to Grace and then to Mulholland and back to Grace.

"Watch after Benita while I go on ahead, darlin'. Don't do nothin' else, just get ready for night and watch after the little girl."

Grace frowned, apparently not understanding. Or maybe she did, for she voiced her own concern that had its roots in Joe's death.

"Papa, promise me you won't get yourself killed."

Wash knew what she meant: *on purpose.*

"Couple of days, we'll be tellin' your mother all about this," he reassured her. "She—"

"Over there by the elderberries, Mr. Baker," interrupted Trey, pointing as he approached on the dun. "What do you suppose . . . ? Lord, that's the other bloodhound, what's left of him."

Just as Wash turned to see for himself, the limbs beyond Isom stirred and popped. Then a roar shook the mountain and splinters flew, and a brute shape broke through like a devil escaping hell. An unstoppable engine of destruction, the grizzly dwarfed Isom, who merely stood in its path and waited.

"Look out!" warned Wash.

He raised his shotgun, but the frightened Appaloosa whirled with him. As the world spun, he saw Trey's dun go wild and the sorrel throw Mulholland to the rimrock. He saw Grace boost Benita into the saddle and the roan jerk free and bolt with the girl. But with his daughter on foot, the most striking thing he saw was a grizzly that could take away forever another child of his.

No!

Wash had the shotgun cocked and ready, but the bear had chosen other prey and fell upon Isom. With a lightning-quick strike of its paw, the grizzly threw the clergyman ten feet and then pounced on him, biting and ripping. Wash wanted to fire but didn't have a shot, not even when the bear seized the screaming man with its jaws and shook him like a terrier would a rat, the tatters of Isom's black cutaway streaming. Dropping him, the bear snatched Isom up by the face and shook him again, the most horrible sight Wash had ever seen. Once more the grizzly released Isom, only to catch him up by the skull and shake him yet again. When it dropped him a third time, the bear left a man shockingly mangled.

As the grizzly fled toward Baldy's cliffs, Wash managed to

fire, and so did Trey. But the shots must have gone wide, for the grizzly never slowed and quickly disappeared beyond hulking boulders.

"Benita!" alerted Grace. "The horse ran with her!"

"I'm after her!"

When Trey cried out, Wash heard the young man's horse recede in the direction from which they had come. Wash didn't waste time with a glance back, for he was reconnoitering and reloading in case the grizzly returned. But as the hoofbeats died away, he turned his face into the moaning wind to identify a muffled voice.

He surveyed the flat, finding Isom motionless and apparently dead. Then the voice came again, and when Wash scanned the rim and saw a hat and a .30-40 rifle near the edge, he took the Appaloosa closer.

"Mulholland?" he called.

"I-god, got nothin' . . . nothin' . . ."

"Where are you?"

""Nothin' . . . Got nothin' . . ."

At the rimrock, Wash dismounted with his shotgun and met Grace running up.

"Where is he, Papa?"

In the V between flat fingers of rock extending over a terrifying drop, he saw hands—white knuckles and knotted digits with dirty nails that clawed at the rim.

"I-god, what's the use?" the voice asked. "My own boy . . . Lost him . . ."

Wash rushed to the near side of the V and Grace to the far side. Two and a half feet separated the fingers of rock, and framed down between were arms and a balding head and boot heels that kicked against a dark forest far below. Mulholland had continued to mutter, and as Wash laid aside his shotgun and he and Grace went to their knees so that they faced one another, Wash processed all that he had heard.

"Begged him . . . come see about me, hurtin' like hell . . . but he wouldn't do it, my own boy . . . lost him . . . I shoot myself a-purpose and he still won't have nothin' to do with me . . ."

The confession of a perpetrator whom Wash had never considered, it convicted Wash for ever believing that Grace had fired the shot. But that was something to brood over later, for Mulholland was about to fall to his death.

We got to kill him, Grace.

The memory came to Wash suddenly, powerfully.

We got to kill Ed Mulholland in a way so's nobody will know.

Here was their chance. After nineteen terrible years, this was the time and place, and Wash looked up at Grace, and she looked at him.

Do it, Grace. If I'm not ever able to, do it for me.

Wash saw the pledge in her eyes, but there was something else that he relived in a memory no less powerful: Mulholland weeping in regret for his role in Joe's death.

Kneeling just as he had at that lonely grave, Wash made his decision, but before he could act, Grace did so on her own.

She reached down and took Mulholland's arm.

It wasn't easy, the two of them dragging an overweight man up on the rim, but finally Mulholland was sprawled, still lamenting the son he had lost in his own way.

"Listen to me, Ed," said Wash. In all these years, it was the first time he had ever addressed Mulholland by his given name. "You got a second chance with him now. It's time you made amends."

Standing, Wash took up his shotgun and looked across the flat. "Brother Isom," he said somberly.

"He's dead, isn't he, Papa?"

Wash retrieved Mulholland's .30-40 and gave it to Grace. "No use you seein' this. Keep a watch for the bear."

A body dreadfully mauled wasn't a memory for anyone to carry, but Wash did what he had to and started across. Isom was stretched out supine at an angle, the head nearer and the feet farther away, and as Wash approached, he found the scene as gruesome as he had imagined. Isom's scalp was peeled back, and disfiguring lacerations from his cheekbone to his throat rendered him unrecognizable. Deep puncture wounds in his chest darkened what little clothing remained, and through a wide rip in his abdomen, Wash could see the poor man's entrails. His limbs, too, had been clawed and chewed, with shredded flesh showing in his thigh, and a bone jutting from his maimed hand.

The hand suddenly twitched.

"Brother Isom?"

Hurrying around to his side, Wash knelt and saw life in the clergyman's eyes. Blood issued from his mouth as he whispered, and what Wash couldn't hear, he read on the trembling lips.

"Two she bears came . . . came out of the woods and mauled them."

"Just lay still, Brother Isom. Just lay still."

Isom clutched Wash's arm. "Judgment . . . Jehovah's agent of judgment."

"We'll get a fire goin', get you warm."

The fingers dug into Wash's skin and the voice gained strength.

"Sin . . . Terrible sin . . . He is faithful and just to forgive. Confess, Isom . . . just confess . . ."

With all of Wash's wrongdoings, he never would have believed that someday he would take the deathbed confession of a man of God. But he did.

A lonely night.

A grieving man.

And a crying newborn who had taken away his wife forever.

But there was more, much more, and Wash listened in shock as Isom told of a pillow in his hand—a feather pillow that smothered until the baby never cried again.

His strength gone, Isom could only move his lips silently now, but the words were plain.

"Forgive me, O Lord . . . Forgive . . ."

Then a strange peace came over his grisly features, and one last whisper passed his lips.

"My Lela . . . Our child . . . They'll never come back to me . . . but I'll go to them."

When the head fell to the side and the pupils dilated, it was over. But for Wash, it was only beginning, for Isom had given him the courage to reach out for his own peace, a calm that had been his to receive ever since the Concho.

Lifting his gaze to the sky, Wash confessed to nineteen years given over to bitterness, and believed again. Now he only needed to right the wrongful shot that had stolen away so much of his life.

CHAPTER TWENTY-ONE

Wash couldn't silence the squeak of his boots or tinkle of his spurs.

The rowels jingled with every step through the talus and on up the scramble over solid rock. The side-by-side barrels of his Colt Model 1878 shotgun, each chamber with a 12-gauge shell with nine .33 caliber pellets, grazed the lichen-covered boulders and added to the sounds so out of harmony with the dusk. Even if a wind hadn't pushed at his back, whatever was up there would know he was coming.

Just as Trey and Tommy had approached the flat with Benita and the roan, Wash had ridden on. From a distance he had seen a moving figure skylined on Baldy's rock-capped summit, and a short ride through scrub oaks had brought him underneath one-hundred-foot cliffs impossible to climb. On the north, the palisades had stretched unbroken for two hundred feet, but on the narrow west flank, Wash had found talus and started up to end the haunting memories once and for all.

He broke over the top to face the full moon, orange and huge, down a rock-and-dirt ridge six feet wide. Left and right, the spine fell away sharply, twenty or thirty feet to the sheer cliffs. The moon glow was beautiful on the residual snow, and had it been another time, Wash would have paused to marvel. But he couldn't, for out of the moon's swollen orb came the grizzly, closing on him with appalling quickness.

Wash thumbed back the hammers of the shotgun and threw

the iron butt plate against his shoulder. He dug his index and middle fingers through the trigger guard and looked down the center rib of the 30-inch barrels. Here was the moment that should have been, nineteen years ago. Here was the rightful aim, the life worth taking, and when he squeezed both triggers, the report seemed to rock not only the mountain but all the years he had wasted.

The animal dropped to the blast and tumbled toward him, but it was up in the same motion and bearing down as swiftly as ever. There was no time to reload. The grizzly was upon him, rearing eight feet and blotting out the moon. If there was a fitting end to Wash's life, this was it, but his renewed faith wouldn't let him give up, and he drove the butt of the shotgun between the monster's eyes so violently that the force broke open the breech.

The grizzly bawled with pain and drew back, giving Wash time to seize another shell and ram it into a chamber. But the impact had damaged the gun, and the breech wouldn't close, and he had nothing left with which to fight as the bear rose up again. Then the crack of a rifle shook the summit and the great bear collapsed, smothering Wash as it crushed him to the ground.

The long, coarse fur and underlying fleece blinded him to everything, and it took a moment for Wash to realize that the grizzly no longer moved. He began trying to extricate himself, terrified that the bear might still be alive, but not until something clutched his arm and pulled did he squirm out.

Uninjured, Wash stood, finding the bear sprawled before a full moon less than an hour old. He turned, expecting to see someone from camp, but instead he was taken aback by the sight of a Mexican boy bathed in moonlight.

"You the one shot?" Wash asked in Spanish.

"*Sí, señor. El oso plateado* is dead."

"Much obliged for that." Wash glanced back. "Full moon's just up good. I'd say you done what you come for."

The muchacho seemed confused.

"You'd be Rosindo," said Wash.

The boy only looked at him.

"Benita's brother," Wash added.

"Benita? What do you—?"

Wash motioned to the west-northwest. "She's over that way, not twenty minutes from here."

"She's alive? My sister's alive?"

"She's been mighty uneasy about you, and about what's goin' to come of her. Told her she's always got a home with us. You too now."

There was joy in the smile and flash of teeth, but suddenly it gave way to excitement in the high, rounded eyebrows.

"Look! Do you see?" asked the boy, pointing over Wash's shoulder.

Wash turned, but saw only the muted gleam of snow under the moon.

"Going up in the sky," added Rosindo.

"Can't see a thing, son. What is it?"

"My *papá*. He's free, and now I'll see him again someday!"

AUTHOR'S NOTE

This novel is based on two actual events in nineteenth-century West Texas: an accidental shooting death, and a bear hunt in which the only documented grizzly ever found in Texas was killed.

After Indians stampeded a Fort Sumner–bound cattle herd at the confluence of the Middle Concho River and Kiowa Creek one night in 1869, trail boss Jim Baker shouted a challenge to a figure he couldn't identity in the dark. When he heard no reply, Baker feared for his life and fired his shotgun, only to discover that he had killed one of his cowhands. "I've had lots of trouble, but nothing ever troubled me like this," Baker recalled. "That was the finest boy I nearly ever saw in my life, and I loved him."

Roberts, W. H. "Bill." SoundScriber interview by J. Evetts Haley, Big Spring, TX, December 21, 1946. N. S. Haley Memorial Library, Midland, TX. Roberts was Baker's nephew.

Striking out on horseback from the Rockpile in the Davis Mountains in November 1899, hunters C. O. Finley and John Z. Means reached the Mount Livermore (Baldy Peak) area with other riders and their hounds. At a partially devoured cattle carcass a mile or so east of the summit, the dogs struck a hot trail, but the spoor frightened the hounds and only a few would pursue. In the brushy head of Merrell Canyon a couple of miles southeast of Livermore, their quarry, presumed to be a black bear, stopped and made a stand. From 125 yards away, Finley and Means opened fire with .30-30 carbines. Wounded, the bear rushed the dogs and fatally mauled one hound before succumbing to additional gunfire. Upon reaching the site, Finley and Means were stunned to learn that they had killed a grizzly. The skull, the only known specimen of *Ursus horriaeus texensis,* is in the Smithsonian National Museum of National History in Washington, D.C. The Smithsonian's holding includes the notation: "Labels, catalogs, and publication all give the date collected as 2 Nov 1890, but letters with the skull from the collectors indicate the correct date was 2 Nov 1899."

Burr, J. G. "A Texas Grizzly Hunt." *Texas Game and Fish* (August 1948). This includes a detailed eyewitness account by Finley.

Evans, Joe M. *Bear Stories.* Privately printed, c. 1955.

Finley, C. O., "Stalking the Unknown." *Pecos News,* July 2, 1965. This includes a detailed eyewitness account by Finley.

Smithsonian National Museum of Natural History. USNM 203198. https://collections.nmnh.si.edu/search/mammals/?ark=ark:/65665/3be797c8fe609431791fddeb3add329fa

BULTO

Dearen, Patrick. *Castle Gap and the Pecos Frontier, Revisited.* Fort Worth: Texas Christian University Press, 2017.

GRIZZLY BEARS

Hittell, Theodore H., *The Adventures of James Capen Adams, Mountaineer and Grizzly Bear Hunter, of California.* Boston: Crosby, Nichols, Lee and Company, 1860.

Journals of the Lewis & Clark Expedition. https://lewisandclark journals.unl.edu/journals

McFarland, Elizabeth Fleming. *Wilderness of the Gila.* Albuquerque: University of New Mexico Press, 1974.

Mills, Enos A. *The Grizzly: Our Greatest Wild Animal.* Boston and New York: Houghton Mifflin, 1919.

Roosevelt, Theodore. *Hunting the Grisly and Other Sketches.* New York: Review of Reviews Company, 1904. Originally published by G. P. Putnam's Sons, 1889, 1894, 1896.

Stevens, Montague. *Meet Mr. Grizzly.* Albuquerque: University of New Mexico Press, 1943.

———. SoundScriber interview by J. Evetts Haley, October 15, 1946. N. S. Haley Memorial Library, Midland, TX.

Thorpe, T. B. *The Mysteries of the Backwoods; or, Sketches of the Southwest.* N.p., n.d.

Wright, William H. *The Grizzly Bear: The Narrative of a Hunter-Naturalist.* New York: Charles Scribner's Sons, 1909.

ABOUT THE AUTHOR

A member of the Texas Literary Hall of Fame, **Patrick Dearen** is the author of twenty-seven books. His ten nonfiction works include *A Cowboy of the Pecos*, *The Last of the Old-Time Cowboys*, and *Saddling Up Anyway: The Dangerous Lives of Old-Time Cowboys*. His research has led to seventeen novels, including *The Big Drift*, winner of the Spur Award of Western Writers of America. His other novels include *When Cowboys Die* (a Spur Award finalist), *Perseverance*, *When the Sky Rained Dust*, *The Illegal Man*, *To Hell or the Pecos*, *Dead Man's Boot*, *Apache Lament*, *Haunted Border*, and *The End of Nowhere*.

A ragtime pianist and wilderness enthusiast who has summited Mount Livermore (Baldy Peak), Dearen lives with his wife, Mary, in Texas. See patrickdearen.com for more information.

The employees of Five Star Publishing hope you have enjoyed this book.

Our Five Star novels explore little-known chapters from America's history, stories told from unique perspectives that will entertain a broad range of readers.

Other Five Star books are available at your local library, bookstore, all major book distributors, and directly from Five Star/Gale.

Connect with Five Star Publishing

Website:
   gale.com/five-star

Facebook:
   facebook.com/FiveStarCengage

Twitter:
   twitter.com/FiveStarCengage

Email:
   FiveStar@cengage.com

For information about titles and placing orders:
   (800) 223-1244
   gale.orders@cengage.com

To share your comments, write to us:
   Five Star Publishing
   Attn: Publisher
   10 Water St., Suite 310
   Waterville, ME 04901